THE SECULARIST

Ashish Talwar

MINERVA PRESS
NEW DELHI
MIAMI LONDON SYDNEY

THE SECULARIST

ISBN 81 7662 094 7

First Published 1999 by
MINERVA PRESS
A1/304 Safdarjung Enclave
New Delhi – 110 029

Printed and bound in India
by BWP&P Ltd., New Delhi

THE SECULARIST

About the Author

Only 30, Ashish Talwar hails from a family of refugees from West Punjab, Pakistan. Born and educated in Delhi, *The Seculartist* is his first novel.

To my mother, at times I forget to thank you for all that you've done.

Preface

It is beyond dispute that the Partition of India was the most painful incident in the human history of the Indian subcontinent. The horrors of that period are firmly etched in the collective memory of those who managed to survive. Unfortunately, my grandfather was a part of that generation and rebuilt his business and life from scratch, but he was fortunate in one sense. He refused to fall in to the traps of the Hindu organisations, which used the refugee camps and colonies in Delhi as a fertile breeding ground to sow their seeds of hatred. The refugees lost their family members and all their worldly possessions and were understandably angry about the Partition. This anger was soon translated by the Hindu fascists into an all consuming hate. It was conveniently forgotten that these Right Wing Organisations were also responsible for the Partition and the bloodbaths that preceded Independence. Their complicity in Mahatma Gandhi's assassination is an indisputable historical fact, leading to a ban on their activities.

I grew up being aware of these historical facts but oblivious to the dangers of communalism. As a school going kid in mid-eighties, I was caught unaware by the aggression that was suddenly unleashed into the country's secular fabric. My most sane friends and relatives began declaring that they were Hindus. I was surprised by their vehement assertions of the dangers to the identity of Hinduism. My sensible arguments that we constituted around seventy-five per cent of the country's population and no minority could ever endanger our identity were ignored. Even the most atheist and miserly among them began contributing liberally for the building of a temple, which they would surely never visit. Much to my relief it expectedly turned out to be a passing phase. But as the Lok Sabha Elections of 1989 came nearer, the stakes for these communal parties increased and the riots began. Cities and towns, which had stayed riot free, even at the time of Partition were enveloped in a frenzy of divisive hatred, reopening the wounds of 1947. I silently witnessed the open challenge to the oneness of India by the assent of these Hindu fascists.

In this garb of political legitimacy a new agenda was put in front of the country. We were told that in order to stay united the country needed a uniform civil code, that refugees, Muslim refugees from neighbouring countries were prone to spread terrorism in our localities and that all secular political parties were *pseudo-secularists*. Still, I silently watched as their canards influenced others and the armies of fascism once again marched albeit this time in white, khaki and black.

And then one fine day, India's nearly one billion people were told that a bolt from the heavens had cleansed their mind of all communal thinking that they were now totally reformed. They had a leader who has a 'mask', one who was secular in thought and action despite having been totally involved in their every fascist scheme for only the past four decades.

It was then that I decided to arise from my nonchalant slumber and fulfil my *pseudo-secularist* duty, I began to write.

Ashish Talwar

Contents

Part One
1947 to 1965

Part Two
1965 to 1972

Part One
1947 to 1965

One

As the afternoon progressed, Lala Khem Chand Sabarwal's discomfort increased. The intense June heat was making the passengers sweat profusely and the whole compartment smelt. The hot gusts of wind coming in from the open windows were so unbearable that due to it the children's noses bled.

When the train started from his hometown, Rawalpindi, his family had the whole coupe to themselves. But as the journey progressed, more and more people had boarded the train and come into their compartment. About four hours into the journey, as the train rolled on through the plains of West Punjab, Khem Chand was at the door of his compartment surrounded by passengers. Even the roof of the train had people on it.

The tension in the compartment was palpable. Almost all passengers had the same worried look and some of the women were crying. Like Khem Chand's family, the other passengers were also travelling with heavy baggage trying to carry as much as possible of their worldly possessions.

As the train once again reduced speed Khem Chand looked out. Several Sikh families were getting in, one of them approached Khem Chand's compartment. He helped an elderly lady climb up the steps. Her eyes were swollen with continuous crying and in her hand she held her holy book. Her son thanked Khem Chand for helping his mother.

Khem Chand questioned him, 'Where are you planning to go?'

'We don't have any plans but we will be happy wherever *Wahe Guru* takes us,' he replied looking skywards.

The Lala nodded his head. He too was a strong believer in fate and the power of the Almighty. His elder son Chander interrupted his thoughts. 'Father, we are very thirsty. Please get some fresh water at the next station,' he said. Entering the coupe Khem Chand picked up a small earthen pot. He glanced at his wife. Even though she was cramped in her seat, Janaki looked beautiful as ever. She was an alacritous homely woman and he loved her dearly. The Lala smiled at her proudly. She was calm despite the tense atmosphere in the compartment.

In his mid-thirties, six feet tall and broad shouldered, Khem Chand was a fair, handsome man. Big, light-coloured eyes and a prominent nose added to his looks. He had the bearing of one born into wealth and seemed to be in total control of his life.

Khem Chand's mind was filled with unanswered questions. The news about Partition had devastated him. His powerful social presence, vast agricultural holdings and a couple of factories were now in a soon-to-be alien country, Pakistan.

The changes had been visible in the past few months. Khem Chand's Muslim friends had become sympathetic but distant. There had been an undercurrent of panic mixed with disbelief among all non-Muslims. Even the robust Sikhs had become somewhat fearful of their future. A few of his Muslim workers had become rude and indifferent.

His oldest employee, Sadiq Mohammed had advised, 'Lala *ji* this is the right time to leave. Many are arming themselves to attack wealthy Hindus like you.' That is when Khem Chand had decided to leave for Delhi. Taking along whatever cash and valuables he could carry and a heavy heart, Khem Chand had locked the doors of his palatial ancestral *haveli*. He had given the keys to a tearful Sadiq and hugged him.

En route to the station many people told him, 'You are leaving at the right time, the panic hasn't spread yet.'

Now looking at the crowded compartment the Lala realised that the panic had already spread. In the past one hour the train had made five unscheduled stops. Among those who boarded the train were farm labourers from Uttar Pradesh who were returning home. 'At least they have a home to go to,' thought Khem Chand. 'I'll have to start all over again.'

The train was slowing down. He looked out and saw that they were approaching a railway station. Remembering his son's request for water he got off the train. Looking for a water tap Khem Chand spotted one a few yards away.

Walking towards it he suddenly realised that the station was deserted. There were no coolies, no tea-sellers, the refreshment stalls were empty and even the railway employees were nowhere to be seen.

The Lala hurried to the tap and as he bent down to fill the pot, he saw some movement from the corner of his eye. All of a sudden he felt a knife at his back.

Turning around he saw two young men. One held the knife and the other had a lathi in his hand.

'Give us all your money and we'll let you go. Otherwise…' demanded the one with the knife.

Khem Chand caught his wrist and punched him on the face. The knife fell from the assailant's hand and he fell down. Catching hold of the other youth, the Lala gave him a couple of blows. But, he freed himself from Khem Chand's grip and swung the lathi hitting the Lala on his head.

Collapsing on the platform, Khem Chand saw the train moving off slowly before he lost consciousness.

Two

Bleary-eyed and tired, Khem Chand got up slowly. His head hurt and it was getting dark. He looked at his wrist but his watch was gone and so were his wallet and the papers he carried inside his shirt.

Khem Chand was worried since he was in an unknown place without money but was relieved that by now his wife and children were in Amritsar at his cousin's house. He looked around. The station was still deserted. Even the reception counter and administrative offices were locked.

Carefully he stepped outside the station. He still couldn't see anyone around but heard moans coming from an upturned rickshaw.

He found an old man lying on his back clutching his stomach. His head and upper body was completely smeared with blood. Khem Chand could make out that the feeble body wouldn't survive much longer. Squatting near the wounded man, he asked, 'Who are you? Why is this place deserted?'

'*Sahab*, I am Ram Singh. I sell tea here,' and then he started coughing. After the spasms stopped, he continued, 'all hell has broken loose here. We were attacked by looters from outside. The Muslims of our village also joined them. Now they have gone to loot trains passing from here.'

'I too was on a train when I was attacked at the platform by a couple of youth.'

'You are very lucky, *Sahab*. If you would have been on that train, you would be dead!' exclaimed the dying man.

'Why is that?' asked Khem Chand worriedly.

'These looters do not leave anyone alive. They enjoy killing as much as they enjoy looting,' the old man replied.

In a panicky voice, the Lala asked, 'My family was on the train. How do I reach them?'

The old man was on the verge of death, 'Down this road is a

railway crossing. From there the road runs parallel to the track. Take this rickshaw. May God help you.' Saying this he breathed his last.

Pedalling the rickshaw, Khem Chand's lips kept moving. He was praying and hoping that his family was safe. And then before him was the train.

In a daze he walked towards it. After a few steps he tripped over something. It was the body of a man, cut in half by swords. Khem Chand got up slowly, not daring to even glance at the other compartments. He reached his own.

The door was open and just beyond it lay the body of the elderly Sikh woman. Her light-coloured clothes completely bloody and eyes open, she still held her holy book. He stepped over her and the body of a young man blocked his path.

With a prayer on his now shivering lips the Lala entered his coupe.

What he saw would haunt him till the day he died. His beloved wife was sprawled on the floor, her half-naked body bathed in blood. His elder son was beside her with a gaping hole in his stomach made by a shotgun fired at point blank range. The younger one was on the compartment berth his brain splattered across it. His head had been repeatedly struck on the hard wooden berth.

Khem Chand started screaming. An uncontrollable torrent of tears started streaming down his checks. Hugging the bodies of his loved ones, he cried his heart out.

After a while, regaining coherency he realised what he had to do. Khem Chand cremated the three members of his family. As the flames devoured them, Khem Chand collapsed cursing his fate, the killers and the whole world around him, which had gone crazy.

Sometime later he heard the wailing of an infant. At first, he dismissed it as his imagination but it continued. Pulling himself up, he moved towards the sound.

Near the engine of the train lay a man in grey uniform of the railways. His body bore many wounds and he was holding a baby to his chest.

Khem Chand squatted next to the wounded man taking the

baby from him.

'I tried to stop them, Lala *ji*. I told them I am a Muslim, please listen to me. But they wounded me. Everybody is dead. *Allah* will never forgive them.'

'But who are you?' asked Khem Chand.

'Don't you recognise me? I am Noora, the nephew of your late manager Ahmed Mian. Please look after my son. Don't think of him as a Muslim.'

'But where should I take this child? Where is his mother, your other relatives?'

'My wife and family were killed last week in Delhi. Take care of my child. *Allah* will always bless you,' saying this the young man died.

Three

Lajwanti had been born into misfortune. Her father had died in an accident months before her birth. During delivery, her mother had also expired and Lajo was born an orphan. It was her mother's brother, Madan, who had adopted her.

He was uncouth and uneducated but a kind-hearted driver. He loved his niece like a daughter and did not marry. Madan brought her up inculcating good values and educating her.

Lajo grew up to be an intelligent and beautiful girl. Ever since she had become sixteen-years-old, every young man in the town was after her. This troubled Madan and whenever he went out of station Lajo was left at a cousin's house a couple of miles from town.

In June 1947, Shekhupura was a communal time bomb ready to explode. Choudhary Karan Singh was a prominent Hindu leader of the town and one of the richest persons around. His only son was a spoilt young man who remained drunk most of the day and throughout the night. Trouble started when Karan Singh's son, Sukhbir, beat up Qasim Khan the son of the local Muslim League leader. They had fought over the charms of a whore and the injuries to Qasim were not serious. In retaliation, several Muslim League workers attacked Sukhbir.

The whole incident was taken as a communal affair and the elders in both communities conveniently forgot that the trouble had started because of a whore. Under normal circumstances, saner heads would have prevailed and the situation would have calmed down. But, with the shadow of Partition upon them, both communities started arming themselves.

Madan feared for his niece and as he had to go to Amritsar, he dropped her off at his cousin's house. The next morning, a Hindu priest was murdered and the situation reached saturation point. In the afternoon, about two hundred outsiders entered the town and encamped in the Masjid.

By night, the whole town erupted with war cries. Muslims on one side and the Hindus and Sikhs on the other. The Sikh Mohalla was attacked but the looters had to retreat with heavy casualties. Frustrated they decided to attack the small villages around Shekhupura.

Lajo was woken up by her aunt. In a panicky voice she said, 'The village is likely to be attacked. They'll leave me as I am old but you are in grave danger. Here is some food hide near the mound half a mile from here. Do not return till all is well.'

Lajo was up in a flash. She pleaded with her aunt to come along but she refused. As soon as Lajo left the village hordes of looters descended. Lajo heard the war cries but didn't look back.

Reaching the small hill she saw that the whole village was burning. Lajo cried for she realised that her aunt was dead and she was alone in this wilderness.

Composing her thoughts she decided that the only way to escape was to reach East Punjab via train. So she decided to reach the railway tracks, catch a train and head for Amritsar and safety.

From the intensity of the heat, Khem Chand realised that it was going to be afternoon soon. He was dead tired and his body was getting numb. Unfamiliar with this part of the country, he had no idea where he was. He just knew one thing, he was going eastward following the railway track. Unable to go any further he sat down for a short rest. He had walked for several hours holding the baby to his shoulder. He had fed the child some mango juice. He was developing a very strong bond with the boy. They had been united by a bizarre twist of fate and he wanted to ensure that the child survived this ordeal. The baby started crying. With the instincts of an experienced father, Khem Chand rocked the boy back to sleep.

He once again thought of his family and tears filled his eyes.

Suddenly, a girl leaped out from behind a tree. Boldly she asked, 'Who are you?'

Khem Chand looked at her carefully, her salwar kameez was soiled. From her appearance he could make out that she was also on the run.

'I am Khem Chand. Who are you? What are you doing here?'

he asked in a calm voice.

'I am Lajwanti from Shekhupura. In the early hours of the day, my town was attacked. I managed to escape and since then I am trying to reach a safe place. Are you from here?'

The Lala narrated his story. When he talked about the murder of his family, the girl's eyes filled with tears. When he told her of the child she took the baby in her arms and sobbed. Khem Chand comforted the girl and asked her, 'I have avoided the railway stations but I don't know my way around this area. Do you know which route is safe?'

The young girl looked at Khem Chand's handsome face. She was very impressed by this brave man who was so calm after all he had gone through.

'Yes, there is an army camp about ten miles from here,' she said.

Getting up Khem Chand said, 'There is no time to waste. This heat is dangerous for the baby. You lead and show me the way.'

The army jawan was amazed at the sight. A tall man wearing a completely tattered shirt covered with dried patches of blood, his eyes bloodshot, carrying an infant against his chest and a young girl over his shoulder walked towards him from the fields. In a tired voice he said, 'Young man, may I see the officer?'

The jawan didn't have to move from his post because the British captain had also seen the man approach the camp.

The Britisher said, 'I am a captain. How can I be of service?'

'My name is Khem Chand Sabarwal. The girl twisted her ankle about three hours back and has become unconscious because of the heat. The infant hasn't been fed for some time.'

The officer took the child from the Lala and a couple of jawans helped Khem Chand in getting the girl off his shoulder. The officer looked at him with respect. 'Sir, you have saved their lives. You are a very brave man,' he said.

The officer could see the sorrow in Khem Chand's eyes.

'At least I managed to save somebody,' he mumbled and then fainted.

They were in the back of an army truck with a dozen other refugees en-route to Amritsar. Khem Chand and Lajo sat next to each other and the baby was sleeping peacefully in Lajo's arms.

Khem Chand looked at her affectionately. He liked this beautiful girl. 'Maybe, I'll find her a good husband one day,' thought Khem Chand.

But Lajo thought of him differently. She was falling in love with this brave and handsome man even though he was twice her age. She also knew that right now he could not reciprocate her feelings. After sometime he'll be mine, Lajo daydreamed.

Khem Chand tapped her shoulder. 'We are about to reach Amritsar,' he said.

Four

Sipping his morning tea, the Lala saw the Red Fort in the backdrop. Despite squalid conditions at the Trans Yamuna refugee camp, looking at the Red Fort he felt secure. It too had been enslaved by the British. Very soon a tricolour would be hoisted on it.

He thought about the past month. It had been the most turbulent period in his life and in the history of the Indian subcontinent. Thousands of people had been massacred, millions were homeless. At some places riots were still going on marring India's Independence Day.

Leaving Amritsar had been difficult for Khem Chand. His cousin Mahendra and his *Bhabhi* Sunita had gone hysterical when they came to know about his family's fate. He had left the child with them after swearing them to secrecy about his origins. The boy was now his son and Khem Chand named him Kabir.

Lajo's uncle was contacted and he came for her. Khem Chand had been sad to see her go as he had become quite attached to her.

After having stayed in Amritsar for a month, Khem Chand decided that it was time to head for Delhi where he had a very dear friend. He borrowed money from Mahendra for the trip. Parting with Kabir had been difficult. At the camp, whenever he saw a child he was reminded of him. Though the pain of losing his family was still acute it was slowly diminishing being replaced by his love for Kabir. The boy was now the focal point in his life. 'I have to build a secure future for him,' thought the Lala.

Just before midnight, the atmosphere was charged with patriotism and hope. Refugees, who had lost their family members and their worldly possessions, at least had something to cheer about. Scores were huddled around the radio. Pandit Nehru was giving his 'Tryst with Destiny' speech. The new Prime Minister's words moved Khem Chand. He realised that along with millions of refugees he too had a tryst with his destiny. The entrepreneur in him also realised that the country needed a resurgence in industry and commerce and many opportunities would crop up.

A couple of days after Independence, Khem Chand decided to visit his friend Naresh Gupta, a wealthy iron merchant. Their friendship was a decade old. He remembered how it had started. Gupta's accountant had embezzled him of a large sum of money and taken off to his native village near Rawalpindi. Through a trader in Lahore, Gupta approached Khem Chand. Not one to refuse a request, Khem Chand had found the offender and managed to extract a major portion of the money. Since then, they had become good friends and established a profitable business relationship. The Lala had come to Delhi in 1943 and stayed at his friend's house. They also corresponded regularly.

Standing outside the huge shop, Khem Chand was surprised to see the changes. The neighbouring shop had been purchased and added to the old one. Inside the shop, dozens of accountants were busy with their account books. Gupta had obviously grown wealthier. As Khem Chand entered the shop, he heard his friend call out 'Lala *ji.*'

Khem Chand was caught in a hug by Naresh Gupta. Dark skinned with blunt features, the fat Gupta was half a foot shorter than Khem Chand. Over the years he hadn't changed much in appearance and like always, he had a couple of *pans* in his mouth.

When they sat down Khem Chand told Gupta about the tragedy that had befallen him. Hearing his friend's narration Naresh wept like a child.

'Do not worry my friend, you shall stay at my house,' he assured Khem Chand.

After a week at Naresh's house in old Delhi, Khem Chand started getting restless. Naresh and his wife were perfect hosts but Khem Chand felt that he had to move on and rebuild his life.

That night at dinner Khem Chand spoke to his friend about his predicament.

'What is the hurry?' asked Naresh.

'I want to get on with things. Its time I started earning a living. Give me any job. I promise I'll do it to the best of my ability.'

Sensing that his friend was adamant Naresh told him about a proposal he had thought of. Several years back, he had started a pipe and utensil fabricating unit in Meerut, in partnership with a British trader. Last year, the partner left for his country selling his share to Naresh. But Naresh had no time to look after the unit. The unit had been reasonably profitable a year back and now it was giving huge losses. The probable reason was mismanagement and skimming by the manager. Naresh's offer was simple. If Khem Chand could turn the unit around he would become a partner without any investment.

Khem Chand accepted his friend's offer with tears in his grateful eyes.

The truck driver dropped Khem Chand just outside Meerut. Khem Chand understood the reason for this. From the truck he could see against the sky, smoke rising from many places as evidence of the communal riots ravaging the town. Khem Chand started into Meerut. Seeing a couple of policemen, he asked for directions. Finding the factory 'N.G. Iron Industries' locked like the other factories in the area, Khem Chand put his bag down and sat on it hoping to see at least one of the employees around. After about an hour, he was awakened from his sleep by the loud screams and the loud chanting of Hindu slogans. Just then, from behind a wall, a boy of not more than ten ran towards him and pleaded, 'Help me, these people will kill me.' The amulet around the boy's neck showed that he was a Muslim. The Lala took the boy's hand and asked him to hide behind the factory. A couple of minutes later, half a dozen men brandishing swords and torches came running towards Khem Chand and enquired who he was. He gave his introduction and the purpose of his being there. Looking at their torch-lit faces he could see wildness in their eyes. These men could easily murder a ten-year-old. One of them spoke, 'Have you seen a ten twelve-year-old boy?'

'No, I haven't,' replied the Lala. 'But why do you ask?'

'He is the son of Sadat Khan, the Muslim goonda. His gang has killed twenty people of our *mohalla*. We'll find him,' replied the man and they hurried on.

After they left, Khem Chand waited for fifteen minutes and then went back to the boy and said, 'Don't worry! I'll take you home.' Picking up the boy, Khem Chand carefully found his way back to the main street. Finding a group of policemen on patrol, he explained what had happened and what Chand had done.

'Had this boy been killed, bloodshed would have escalated beyond control. We'll get him back to his father. Thank you very much,' said the inspector.

'I want to meet the boy's father,' said Khem Chand.

'But that might be dangerous, his father hates Hindus,' warned the Inspector.

'I'll be the judge of that,' the Lala said in a stern voice.

The inspector gave a shrug and motioned him to follow them.

After walking for about twenty minutes through a maze of unlit streets, suddenly two men appeared out of the shadows.

'What is it?' they asked the Inspector. Both were holding guns and were guarding their *mohalla*. 'This man, has rescued Sadat Khan's son and wants to meet him,' replied the policemen pointing towards Khem Chand.

The transformation in the men's attitude was visible. They hugged the boy and then Lala was asked to follow them. After a few yards, they turned into another street and Khem Chand was amazed to see the activity. Several men armed to the teeth sat on cots, swords and lathis were standing against the wall.

'Who is this?' they asked.

One of Khem Chand's guides explained. The men looked at him with respect and asked him to come into a small well-lit house. In the verandah of the house, a heated argument was going on. A middle-aged man, six feet tall and a scar across his right check was arguing with a man of the same age. But the other man was bearded and just above five feet.

'Never, never! You Congress *walas* are all the same. You do not know a thing about the enmity between Hindus and Muslims. I don't want peace. Let them kill my son. I'll massacre a hundred Hindu boys even if he is returned. They want to grab our property. Even the government and police are afraid of me, that is why they sent you here.'

Just then, the boy ran to the taller of the men and shouted, '*Abba*'.

Sadat picked him up and hugged him, thanking his Lord. One

of the men went up to him and whispered in his ear. Sadat Khan approached Khem Chand, shook his hand and asked him to sit. 'Get us some tea,' he shouted to one of his men.

As the three of them finished tea, Sadat thanked Khem Chand again and said in a gruff voice, 'I don't want to owe any favours to a Hindu. Ask anything from me and then please leave.'

The Lala had expected this gesture from Sadat Khan. He took a look at the bearded man who had introduced himself as Sattar Ahmed, a Congress leader who was also a member of the Constituent Assembly. He looked straight into Sadat Khan's eyes and started speaking, 'Two months ago I started for Delhi from my native town, Rawalpindi. On the way, my wife and two sons were brutally murdered by Muslim looters. My wife was probably raped before she was killed. I cremated them, performing all the rites by myself, all alone.

I am not even sure of the name of the village where I cremated them. Then, I found a young Muslim man holding his infant son to his chest. He gave me the baby before he died. Today, in your town, I found several Hindu looters looking for your son, wanting to murder him. All these incidents made me think. Looters are looters and not Hindus or Muslims. They are not men but animals. Their only religion is looting. It is very sad that we had to experience this tragic Partition in our lifetime. I had money and name in Rawalpindi. I had to leave it all behind. Don't you think losing all this makes me mad? But being a rational man, I realised that it wasn't the fault of a community but those animals disguised as men. Had the looters found your son and not known who he was, would they have killed him? Does he look like a Muslim? Do I look like a Hindu? You tell me what a Muslim or a Hindu looks like. Sattarbhai has brought you a proposal of peace. But you want to kill Hindus and they want to kill your people. Where will this end? How long will this mayhem continue?'

All through Khem Chand's speech Sadat Khan had just stared at him. At the end of it, he got up and walked off.

Sattar Ahmed looked up at Khem Chand in awe, 'You have guts, sitting here and talking to him like that. Let's pray that your words make him change his stand.'

Khem Chand poured himself some more tea. Tired and

hungry, he dozed off in the chair itself.

After a while Khem Chand felt somebody shaking him and he opened his eyes. Sadat stood in front of him with a broad smile. 'You are a great man and also a very brave one. I am going to the peace meeting. *Inshallah*, there will be peace in Meerut,' said Sadat Khan.

Khem Chand smiled back and slept again.

The transformation was unbelievable. Within a week after the peace meeting had ended successfully, the town was once again back to normal. Shops reopened, rickshaws started plying again, Meerut once again looked like a typical North Indian town.

Five

Lala *ji's* factory was under full production in a week. The factory's dishonest manager had been summoned and promptly asked to resign. He had accepted this quietly knowing the Lala's proximity to the dangerous Sadat Khan and the influential Sattar Ahmed. Most of the labourers too knew this and worked diligently. Khem Chand's customers were in Meerut and the nearby towns. He toured the area extensively and since, his was the only factory working on full production, he made many new customers. Refugees from Pakistan were settling in towns like Meerut, Saharanpur and Ghaziabad. Many of them opened shops and Khem Chand made some of them his dealers.

In six month's time Khem Chand was back in Delhi trying to convince Naresh Gupta to set up a larger factory in Ghaziabad, near Delhi. Naresh came from a long line of old Delhi traders and wasn't comfortable investing in manufacturing units. But now, before him was an experienced and brilliant entrepreneur who had turned a losing business into a flourishing enterprise requiring expansion. He agreed and soon the second unit of 'N.G. Iron Industries' was on its way.

For Khem Chand, time was now the most precious commodity. He was continuously on the move in his new car monitoring his factories and meeting his dealers. Kabir was living with him and was about two years old. He was the joy of Khem Chand's life. Whatever little time they had together was spent in Khem Chand hugging the boy or just staring at his cherubic face. He had also decided on how to raise the boy. Kabir would be given religious training in both Hindu and Muslim faiths. The Lala hoped that his adopted son would become a symbol of religious tolerance. And, with that intent he had purposely hired a Muslim *ayah* to rear the child.

The only thing troubling Khem Chand was his partner's failing health. Naresh had been bedridden for a month, ailing from a disease, which had not been diagnosed. He was tense on the morning of 1 June 1949 when a messenger informed him of Gupta's death the previous evening.

On his arrival at Gupta's residence he found out that the last rites had already been performed and when Khem Chand was consoling the bereaved mother and wife, Naresh's brother Ashok Chand Gupta gestured that he wanted to talk to him.

'We now own N.G. Iron Industries. You hand over the keys and leave the factories.'

'But I am the joint owner,' Khem Chand replied.

Ashok raised his voice, 'Rubbish. You are just a manager and I am terminating your service. My brother took pity on your refugee status and helped you. Now on his death, you claim to be a partner. Shame on you! If you do not leave quietly, you'll be kicked out.'

Not wanting to create a scene, Khem Chand left.

Three days later, a couple of lawyers accompanied by several men were at Khem Chand's small house behind the factory in Meerut. The older of the two lawyers spoke, 'We represent the Gupta family. You are to hand over possession of the two factories and vacate this house. If you do not do so, we'll be forced to initiate legal action against you.'

'I will accept the legal heirs of my deceased friend as my partners. I have no written documents but I have possession of the units. These six, seven *goondas* do not frighten me. I have a double barrel gun with me and it is always kept loaded. Do not show me muscle power. I survived the Partition. So, I can easily survive anything, fools like Ashok Gupta or you can do,' thundered Khem Chand.

The lawyers hurriedly handed him a legal notice on behalf of Ashok Gupta and left.

In the following month, Khem Chand hired a lawyer who informed him that his legal position wasn't sound and he was likely to lose the business. Khem Chand's attempts to contact Naresh Gupta's widow were also unsuccessful. Contemplating his next course of action, the Lala was sitting in his verandah on a rainy July evening. There was a knock on his door. Opening it Khem Chand recognised Naresh's septuagenarian driver Sant

Ram. 'Come in Sant Ram *ji*. What are you doing here?' he asked.

Sitting on a stool, the rain-drenched driver was soon sipping tea.

'Sahab, I need your help. Ashok Sahab has kicked me out and I have no money. I need money to reach my native village in Bihar,' pleaded the old man.

'Do not worry. You will have the fare to reach your village. Spend the night here and tomorrow morning I'll personally take you to the railway station,' said Khem Chand compassionately.

'Lala *ji*, there is one matter I have to tell you about. I know Ashok Sahab wants to take your factories. But Naresh *ji* always spoke about how you saved him from ruin. Naresh Sahab made a will three months before he died. You should see that will. Maybe he left you your share.'

'Naresh *Bhaiya* has left hundred per cent of N.G. Iron and the Civil Lines bungalow to this man. I do not believe this. I will contest this will, come what may,' threatened Ashok. The offices of Lawson and Co., one of the most famous solicitors of Delhi, were full of late Naresh Gupta's relatives and friends.

'Please calm down,' pleaded an elderly man of the Gupta clan, but Ashok gave him an angry look.

Indifferent to Ashok's outburst, the Lala's eyes filled with tears. Naresh had been a true friend to the last and Khem Chand could never hope to repay his friend's last generosity. Ashok continued his cursing and threatening until a stern voice was heard.

'Sit down, young man and behave yourself.' It was Mr Lawson.

Ashok sat down and the Englishman continued, 'Understand one thing, the property and factories left to Mr Khem Chand constitute just one-fifth of Late Sh Naresh Gupta's assets.

If you choose to contest this will, four-fifths of the estate, of which the beneficiary is your family, will also not be transferred in your names. Now tell me, do you accept this will?'

Ashok looked around him. His relatives were giving him angry looks. He nodded his head, 'I accept it.'

By 1955, Lala Khem Chand's business had grown manifold.

He acquired four additional units in Uttar Bharat and Punjab. N.G. Iron Industries had grown 20 times in the last six years. His keen sense of business had made him acquire a big sugar mill near Meerut. He named it Kabir Sugar Mills and it was now giving a good profit. His home was the spacious Civil Lines bungalow Naresh Gupta had left him. It's interior was reminiscent of the palaces of Maharajas. Khem Chand had exceeded the wealth he had lost eight years back.

On 15 August, Khem Chand organised a big function at his bungalow. Sattar Ahmed, now a Union Minister, was the Chief Guest. Several members of Parliament and the city's leading businessmen were among the guests who also included Khem Chand's business dealers and friends. Kabir now a smart eight-year-old was the centre of attraction. His bearing and manners were appreciated by all. The party ended with Sattar Ahmed's speech in which he spoke with great pride about Khem Chand as a businessman who had rebuilt his life and as a human being who saved hundreds of lives by stopping the riots.

Almost all the guests had left when a middle-aged man with a short young man approached Khem Chand. He recognised the man as R C Khanna, a dealer of N.G. Iron Industries.

'Lala *ji*, this is my son Sanjeev. He has just finished his graduation'.

The boy touched Khem Chand's feet, 'Sir, I am a great fan of yours. My father talks a lot about you. I feel great meeting you finally. You are an inspiration to all refugees.'

Khem Chand was tired. He patted the boy on his shoulder and turned away.

'Sir.'

'What is it son?' asked Khem Chand.

'Sir, I have a few business ideas, I want to discuss with you.'

The eagerness and confidence in the young man's voice was pleasantly surprising for Khem Chand.

'Come to my office tomorrow at 10 o'clock sharp,' he replied.

Sanjeev Khanna's proposals opened the Lala's eyes to the corporate world. He was surprised to learn that companies smaller than N.G. Iron Industries and Kabir Sugar Mills were listed on the stock exchange. He also learned that the production of certain chemicals was very profitable and their process was closely related to the sugar industry. But the biggest revelation for him was that he was probably the only businessman of this level who was operating solely on his own resources. He had no shareholders, no debt, not even an overdraft.

Three hours into the enlightening discussion, Khem Chand spoke, 'Sanjeev, I want you to be the head of the soon-to-be-formed Kabir and Co. Ltd.'

Six

In the next eight years Kabir and Co. Ltd. rose to become one of the biggest industrial houses in North India. It's three main subsidiaries, Kabir Sugars Ltd., N.G. Iron Industries Ltd. and Kabir Chemicals Ltd., were market leaders in their respective fields. Competent managers run the business efficiently and they were monitored by Sanjeev Khanna who was now an invaluable asset for Khem Chand.

Khem Chand had donated Rs One Lac to the Punjab Refugee Welfare Association and they held a function in Amritsar to thank him. He agreed because he felt a kinship with the refugee who were likely to be present and he also knew that he was an inspiration for many of them. Addressing the hundreds present, Khem Chand spoke about the dreaded day his family had been massacred. He also used the opportunity to thank the local people who had taken the refugees in and helped them integrate into the community.

At the end of the programme, Khem Chand was sitting with his cousin Mahendra Kumar, now a big dealer of Kabir and Co.'s products, and several of the organisers. From the corner of his eye he saw a woman in white quietly approaching them. She was dressed in a white salwar kameez, a *chunni* of the same colour over her head. She stopped in front of him. 'You forgot me Lala *ji*,' she said. Khem Chand looked at her beautiful face carefully and into the dove like eyes, 'How can I ever forget? You are Lajo, aren't you?'

The widowed Lajo's eyes lit up as she gave him a big smile.

The next day they were both at Mahendra's house talking their hearts out, recounting the last sixteen years of their lives. Lajwanti had been married off months after her arrival from Pakistan. Her husband had been a small trader who had died a few months after the marriage. Her in-laws had deemed her an unlucky wife and she was made to leave their house. She had rebuilt her life by completing her studies and was now a school teacher. She didn't have any surviving relatives as her uncle had passed away the previous year.

'I read in the newspapers that your son is a brilliant student, sure to be as successful as the father. I suppose you kept the child.'

'Yes, but he doesn't know about his origins. He thinks he is my son,' replied Khem Chand.

'But you should tell him now. He's old enough,' said Lajo.

'I send him to the Mosque every Friday. His *ayah* Shahida tells him of the Koran's teachings – when he becomes older I will tell him.'

'You are a great man, Lala *ji*. After what happened you have raised a Muslim as your son,' saying this Lajo got up and hugged Khem Chand.

Khem Chand felt her voluptuous body close to him. He had accepted her hug as a friend but now his body was feeling the body of a beautiful young woman next to it. He broke the embrace, embarrassed by his arousal.

'I haven't told you everything about my son.' Smiling Lajo sat down again.

The next day they parted sadly. They both stood in front of each other silently looking into each other's eyes. Khem Chand broke the eye contact stepping in the train he said, 'Why don't you come to Delhi to meet Kabir?'

Lajo smiled at him, 'You tell him about me and if he wants I'll surely visit Delhi.'

Kabir Sabarwal was now a handsome sixteen-year-old. He had finished his schooling and was now awaiting admission into a college. He was almost six feet tall, broad shouldered and had nice features. Kabir worshipped his father and was a dutiful son. He had been tutored in both Hindu and Islamic faiths. Being religious, he regularly visited the Temple. He resented going to the Mosque every Friday, but he loved and respected his father too much not to obey him. Being an intelligent student he was appreciated and respected by his friends. Numerous girls were attracted to Kabir but he had eyes only for an Anglo-Indian girl Mary Verma. His eyes constantly followed her but he never gathered the courage to speak to her.

Kabir's love for Mary was so secretive that even his best friend Shakeel didn't know about her. Shakeel was Kabir's friend since childhood and matched him in intelligence and looks. He kept pestering Kabir to tell him about the girl he loved. But Kabir never told him. The only difference between them was that Shakeel was always surrounded by girls and Kabir kept to himself. They made a handsome pair and unknown to either of them, Mary also liked one of them.

Sanjeev Khanna was suggesting a new diversification. 'Anticipating a foodgrain shortage the government is likely to take many measures for increasing production. Subsidies maybe in the pipeline for those industries, which can grant impetus in achieving this object. Use of fertilisers was expected to increase manifold. The government will itself advertise for usage of fertilisers and shall distribute them on its own. A unit of capacity... 'Lala *ji*, Lala *ji*, have you heard a word of what I have said?'

'Sorry, Sanjeev,' apologised the Lala.

'We'll discuss this later as your thoughts are preoccupied,' Sanjeev replied, leaving the office.

As Sanjeev closed the door Khem Chand realised that this was, perhaps, the first time he had lost his concentration while listening to a proposal from his most brilliant employee.

Maybe it's my age thought Khem Chand. But he himself knew better. Since his return from Amritsar, Lajo had completely taken over his mind. Lajo's beautiful face, her eyes, her smile and the youth of her body kept him awake at nights. 'Is she interested in me?' The Lala questioned himself.

There was just one way he could find the answer. He reached for his letter pad and started writing.

The Delhi Railway Station was teeming with people but the Lala's eyes searched the doors of the incoming train for just one figure. Lajo stepped on to the platform tentatively. Seeing Khem Chand come towards her, she gave him a small smile. Khem Chand immediately felt that she was tense and hesitant. His driver took her suitcase and Khem Chand her arm.

'Don't worry. I have furnished a house for you in Patel Nagar and got you a job in a nearby school.'

'All the worries I had vanished when I read your letter,' replied Lajo.

The small house in Patel Nagar had been adequately furnished and Lajo liked it. As the servant made tea, Khem Chand started describing the job he had arranged for her.

'I don't want to know. Whatever decision you have taken is good enough for me,' Lajo assured him.

As the sun set Khem Chand got up to leave, Lajo came into his arms.

'I hope you are happy coming to Delhi leaving your house in Amritsar,' Khem Chand said softly caressing her hair.

Lajo looked deeply into his eyes, 'I haven't come to Delhi for this house or the job. I have come because I have been in love with a man who saved my life years ago. And each year my longing for that man has increased.'

'I am 51, at least 20 years older than you,' said the Lala.

'My love for you transcends all barriers of age.'

'I too love you, Lajo,' admitted Khem Chand kissing her passionately.

The next morning Lajo was introduced to Kabir as a cousin of his mother. She hugged the boy affectionately commenting on his good looks. Kabir smiled at her compliment but he felt threatened by her presence. Lajo stayed for lunch and the Lala showed her the bungalow. Kabir's long standing *ayah,* Shahida Begum, sensed that they were in love. In her fifteen years of service, this was the first time Khem Chand had brought a woman to the house.

Late at night, after Lajo had left and Kabir was in his room, Shahida went to the Lala's room.

'What is it, Shahida Bibi?'

'She is a lovely woman, Lala *ji.'*

'Yes, she is Shahida. But why are you mentioning this?'

'I just felt nice seeing her here.

'So did I, so did I,' smiled the Lala.

The very next day, Khem Chand reached Lajo's house early in the morning.

'Hurry up and come along. I have a surprise for you.'

'What is the surprise?' asked Lajo.

'Don't ask, the priest is waiting at the temple.'

'What priest? What temple? What are you talking about?' asked Lajo.

'We are getting married. Hurry up.'

Lala Khem Chand and Lajwanti were married in a quiet religious ceremony. A week later, Khem Chand held a magnificent reception at his house. The talk of the party was the lovely bride and almost everybody congratulated Khem Chand. He himself was troubled because Kabir had quietly disappeared from the scene, leaving a note that he was studying at a friend's house.

At his shop, Ashok Chand Gupta read about Khem Chand's wedding in the newspaper. The reporter had also dwelt on the fact that his first wife and two children had been killed in 1947. Reading the news made Ashok go into a foul mood causing him to shout angrily at his employees on trivial matters. In walked one of his regular customers, R N Mehta.

'You are in a bad mood, Gupta *ji*,' he said, sitting down.

'It is all because of refugees like you.'

'Gupta *ji*, we are no longer refugees but citizens of Delhi. Anyway, what is troubling you?'

'It is that bastard, Khem Chand Sabarwal. My brother made him a big industrialist, now he doesn't even remember us.'

'You are mistaken about Lala *ji*, he is an honourable man. I have known him since Rawalpindi, we were then his tenants. I still remember the day he left for Delhi with his wife and two sons. We were lucky to have left a couple of days later. Otherwise my family would have been killed too,' said Khanna.

'Wife and two sons, but didn't he have three sons?' questioned Ashok.

'No, just two sons, both were killed.'

'But he has a son living with him. Was his wife expecting when she left for Delhi?'

'No, she wasn't,' replied Khanna.

'Then from where has this son come,' thought Ashok.

At four p.m. Ashok Chand Gupta was in the cabin of Tarun Banerjee, a young investigator of International Investigations (P)

Ltd., a well known detective agency in the capital.

Gupta told Tarun Banerjee about the matter he wanted to investigate.

'One thing is for sure,' said Gupta. 'Kabir Sabarwal is not the biological son of Lala Khem Chand Sabarwal. Now, it is your job to get conclusive proof and investigate his origins.'

'Don't worry about that, Mr Gupta. We will find out everything possible about this boy,' assured Banerjee.

'Do you need any information pertaining to this case?' asked Gupta.

'Yes, of course,' said Banerjee. 'Tell me all you can about Lala Khem Chand. Whether he has any living relatives or not, any friends from Rawalpindi who may still be around, where he first stayed when he came to Delhi?'

Gupta started telling the investigator all that he knew about Khem Chand.

Part Two

1965 to 1972

Seven

Kabir's admission into one of Delhi's premier colleges St. Stephens, was a great source of joy and pride for Khem Chand. As any proud father would, he told everybody how he did not have to use any influence for his brilliant son's admission. Kabir was also overjoyed about it. The love of his life, Mary Verma and his best friend, Shakeel, had also been accepted in the same college. Kabir's life was once again in a familiar groove and constantly before his eyes was the pristine beauty of Mary.

Every day his primary aim of going to college was seeing her. She looked even more beautiful in her different outfits no longer having to wear the school uniform. He still hadn't had the guts to tell her of his true feelings. Meanwhile, Shakeel had a new girlfriend every month and constantly chided his friend for being so shy.

'You are a handsome and intelligent boy,' he said, 'When you spoke so well at the inter-college debate, lots of girls were talking about you. When do you plan to grow up?'

Kabir answered with a shy smile.

But Kabir's near perfect life had been shattered by his father's decision to remarry. He was devastated for he thought that he was no longer the centre of his father's life. Nothing was further from the truth than Kabir's feelings towards his father. Khem Chand and Lajo talked late into the night about Kabir's future.

Khem Chand constantly spoke about how he wanted Kabir and Co. to be bigger and more powerful by the time Kabir joined it.

Lajo tried to be extra nice to her stepson but was always snubbed by him. Shahida always told him not to be indifferent towards Lajo, but Kabir refused to listen and they had heated arguments over the issue.

Khem Chand also noticed his son cold-shoulder Lajo. But he kept his counsel knowing that admonishing Kabir would take him further away from home.

As life at home became more and more uncomfortable, Kabir spent most of his time with Shakeel. Shakeel was sympathetic. 'There is no need for you to feel embarrassed. My father married a second time when I was ten, I too felt very bad. The worst part is that now I have a stepbrother with whom I have to share everything. However, I have come to like my stepmother. Maybe you will also like yours.'

'Never,' stressed Kabir.

'Well, there is a silver living in this dark cloud,' said Shakeel. 'After my father remarried, for some time I got whatever I demanded. You should do the same. Just ask for bigger toys. Get smart.'

That night at the dinner table Kabir was at his best behaviour. He was respectful towards Lajo and engaged in small talk with her. Khem Chand and Shahida were relieved. Kabir's disrespect towards his stepmother had receded and his changed attitude demonstrated that he had started liking her.

The next morning Kabir was in front of his father. 'Daddy, I would like a personal car for myself.'

'But, son, we have three cars and they are yours too,' said Khem Chand.

'No. What I mean is, I want a car I can drive. You know I am a safe driver.'

Khem Chand stood up and kissed his son's forehead, 'OK, tomorrow your new car will be at the door.'

'Wow! What a fantastic car,' exclaimed Shakeel admiring the red convertible Chevrolet.

'I just listened to your advice and asked for a big toy,' said Kabir.

'This isn't a toy my friend,' Shakeel said. 'This magnificent automobile is going to transform our lives. We have become the most desirable boys in the University. We just have to snap our fingers and the girls will do anything in exchange for a ride with us.'

'You have a one-track mind. Aren't there others in Delhi University who have cars?' asked Kabir.

'Yes, there are many who have personal cars. But none of

them are handsome Stephenians like us,' Shakeel replied.

Shakeel proved to be right as almost the whole college congratulated Kabir on his new car. After several days the excitement wore off and life seemed to drag on.

As Kabir was waiting for his friend in the college café, in walked Shakeel accompanied by two girls. Kabir felt a shortness of breath. One of them was Mary Verma, looking resplendent in her white printed blouse and short skirt.

'Hello, Kabir. How are you?' She greeted him. Her soft voice was the music his ears had longed to hear.

'I am fine, thank you', he replied formally.

As they sat down Shakeel spoke, 'You know Mary and this is Padma Banerjee you must have seen her around.' After Kabir had wished the dusky Bengali beauty, Shakeel continued, 'They want to see how good a driver you really are. So on Sunday we are all going to risk our precious lives and travel to your favourite ruins in Delhi, the Tughlakabad Fort. Don't refuse and break their hearts.' Speechless, Kabir nodded his head.

'And get that wonderful cook of yours to pack lunch as we are going to have a picnic in the ruins,' said Shakeel winking at his friend.

It was a glorious Sunday afternoon when they reached Tughlakabad. As they explored the ruins, Kabir impressed the girls with his knowledge of the fort's history. Shakeel entertained them with his amusing anecdotes. 'She looks even more beautiful when she laughs,' Kabir thought looking at Mary. Hungry, they devoured the sumptuous lunch prepared by Kabir's cook.

They got up to leave and Shakeel put his arms around both the girl's leading them to the car. Kabir felt angry seeing his friend's arm around Mary's shoulder. He realised that Shakeel was behaving as usual.

'Shakeel will have to behave himself when he comes to know about my feelings for her,' Kabir thought. He was sure Mary too was interested in him proof of which was her desire to go on this picnic. 'Next time we go out, I'll talk to her,' he decided.

The next day Kabir arrived at a small party in Hindu College hostel. Shakeel had also been invited but could not make it, as he was busy. Without his friend the party was a monotonous affair for Kabir. He didn't know most of the hundred odd boys present.

Awaiting an opportunity to slip out quietly, he felt a tap on his shoulder.

'Mr Kabir Sabarwal, isn't it?'

'Yes,' he replied turning around. It was Rajesh Pahwa, son of a prominent Hindu Leader and President of the Delhi Unit of the Indian Students Sangh. He was a diminutive boy. Five and a half feet in height, thin with a slightly dark complexion.

'I am very happy that you are here without your Muslim friend,' said Rajesh.

'Shakeel is busy elsewhere. But you know his name. So why call him just a Muslim?' enquired Kabir.

'Because they are all the same whatever they are named,' replied the student leader.

'I see that the Indian Students Sangh's views are consistent with those of the Swatantra Sangathan and the Indian Lok Sangh.'

'We are a political organisation and the students wing of the I.L.S. but the Swatantra Sangathan is a social organisation which only guides us. Every Hindu should be a voter of our party and every refugee should be an active supporter. We refugees lost everything in the Partition. Your mother and brothers were killed, weren't they?' asked Rajesh trying to convince Kabir.

'They were. But in a diverse country like ours, only the Congress's policy can work,' argued Kabir.

'If you keep thinking like this, I am sure you will regret it. One day your friend will stab you in the back, mark my words.'

Eight

At the dinner table, father and son were at their debating best.

'I will always support a political party whose ideology is in conformity with mine,' said Khem Chand.

Kabir was trying to convince his father to build relations with opposition parties. 'But why just the Congress, why not the I.L.S. or any other opposition party?'

'The Indian Lok Sangh is a power in the hands of the Swatantra Sangh and the S.S. is as much responsible for the Partition as the Muslim League. How can I ever support them?' said Khem Chand, starting to lose patience.

'The I.L.S. is a national party. An industrialist like you should not take sides. They are likely to come to power in Delhi and maybe a couple of other states,' insisted Kabir.

'I don't care if they come to power at the centre. Kabir and Co. will never support those fanatics,' said Khem Chand raising his voice.

'Enough both of you. We are sitting here to have dinner. So, please have it,' said Lajo intervening before either of them could prolong the debate.

Sitting in the college lawn, Kabir asked Shakeel, 'For the last three days I have not seen you in college. If you bunk any more you are likely to fail.'

'Our reasons for coming to college are different. You are here just to study while I want to enjoy,' said Shakeel. 'I have a beautiful new girl friend.'

'Which poor girl is it this time?' questioned Kabir.

'Why don't you find one for yourself? At least then you won't be so envious and frustrated,' teased Shakeel.

'Don't worry, next time we go out, I'll introduce her to you'.

'That will be the day,' said Shakeel laughingly.

After attending one lecture Shakeel bunked the next one. As

there was time for the third one to start, Kabir decided to find him and force him to attend. He looked around the college but he was nowhere to be seen. 'If he is on a date he must have gone to the Ridge,' thought Kabir. The Ridge was an ideal dating spot for young couples who used the dense shrubbery to their advantage.

In the Ridge's parking area he spotted Shakeel's cycle with the distinctive bright coloured basket on its handle. 'You are in for a surprise my friend,' Kabir smiled at his thoughts. After a short search he heard Shakeel's inimitable voice from behind a shrub. Moving as noiselessly as possible, Kabir looked from between the leaves. He saw Shakeel with a girl in his arms and he was kissing her passionately. The girl had her back to him and he couldn't make out who she was. After a minute they stopped kissing and he saw his friend lower his head.

Kabir got the worst shock of his life. The girl with her arms around his friend, arching her back in ecstasy, was none other than Mary.

Trembling, he retraced his steps. Sweating profusely and with tears streaming down his checks, he managed to get back to the car. His brain seemed to explode as anger and disgust overtook any other feeling he had ever had. With numb fingers he switched on the ignition. Not wanting to go home he started driving towards New Delhi. Reaching the India Gate lawns he parked his car in a secluded place under a tree. Crying loudly he started hitting his head on the steering wheel.

An old beggar tapped at the car window. Kabir looked up, embarrassed at his own state he quickly started the car and sped off. Wiping his face with a hanky he realised that he had been crying for almost two hours and there seemed to be no tears left.

His love for Mary had been replaced by an intense hatred. 'I have wasted a lot of time. I could have had a dozen girls,' he thought. He also remembered Rajesh Pahwa's words about Shakeel.

'I will show them,' he said loudly.

The brothels of G.B. Road in Old Delhi were known for their notoriety throughout India. Through his car window Kabir could see the scantily clad girls calling out at passers-by from their balconies. He parked his car opposite one such brothel and got out. Lacking the confidence to cross the road and enter it, he started strolling aimlessly. A short bald man approached him.

'Come with me, *Sahab*. I will find you the best girls in G.B. Road.'

Nodding his head, Kabir started following the pimp.

The long dingy staircase smelt of tobacco and alcohol. Kabir had to hold his nose to avoid these unfamiliar smells. The pimp laughed, 'You don't drink.'

'Yes, I have never been a disciple of Bacchus,' replied Kabir.

'Who is this Bacchus?' asked his illiterate companion.

'He is the Greek God of Wine.'

'Then you should be his devotee. Your swollen eyes tell me that you are very sad. One peg and you will forget everything,' advised the pimp.

They were in a large well-lit room surrounded by about twenty girls. They wore all kinds of different dresses revealing a lot of their bodies, heavy make up adorned their faces. In the centre was a big sofa and on it sat a dark fat woman of about fifty. One girl was combing her hair while another was pressing her feet. She was obviously the Madame of the brothel and seeing them called out, 'Avinash come, sit here.'

The pimp motioned Kabir to follow him and they sat on chairs near the Madame. The girls looked at Avinash, the pimp, with disgust. To Kabir they gave inviting smiles. One of them winked at him.

'This is my customer. Show him your best girls. But first we are very thirsty and need something to drink,' said Avinash. The Madame gestured to a slim young girl in a saree. She returned with a tray, which contained a large whisky bottle, soda and a couple of glasses. She made a drink for Kabir.

'Believe me, you need it,' said the pimp. Taking the glass, Kabir stared at it for a few seconds deciding whether to drink it or not. The girl standing next to him put it to his lips advising him to drink it slowly. Not wanting to show his inexperience, Kabir gulped it quickly. His throat seemed to burn and he started to cough. Avinash laughed and making an obscene gesture of triumph asked the girl to give them another round of drinks.

Thoroughly intoxicated, Kabir staggered into the room in the arms of a beautiful young whore. Closing the door, she made him lie on the bed. She undressed. It was the first time he had seen a naked woman. He looked at her made up face and remembering Mary, started crying. The whore opened his trousers but the day's events and the memory of his lost love had their affect.

'You are just a small boy,' she laughed at his lack of arousal.

Seeing her laugh Kabir shouted, 'Shut up, you slut.'

But she continued. Suddenly angry Kabir buttoned up his trouser and getting up slapped the girl on her cheek. Stung by his behaviour she too raised her voice, 'Get out, little boy.' Her reply further angered him and he slapped her harder. The girl's lip started bleeding. Stark naked she opened the door and shouted for help. A couple of big tough looking men entered the room. One of them punched Kabir in the stomach and he went down. The other gave him a couple of kicks in the stomach. Then they both picked him up, carried him down the stairs and threw him on the pavement outside the building.

Kabir picked himself up. He didn't feel any pain as the alcohol had dulled his senses, but his feet would not stop shaking. His purse and wristwatch were missing, only his car keys were left. He drove slowly trying to focus on the road. He felt humiliated by all that had transpired at the brothel. 'It is all because of Mary and Shakeel,' he thought.

He knew he couldn't go home in this state and had to wash up somewhere. There was a tea stall outside his college, which could be used by him.

As he parked his car alongside the stall he saw a couple sitting on a bench next to the stall. Rubbing his eyes he looked again. It was Shakeel and Mary. Shakeel also saw him and taking Mary's hand came upto the car.

'Hi, Kabir. Meet my new girlfriend,' he said. Mary smiled happily.

Kabir didn't say anything and just stared at him.

'We had our college play rehearsal. That is why we are still here. What is this smell? Have you been drinking?' asked Shakeel. Controlling his tears, Kabir started the car.

'Stop, Kabir. What's wrong with you?'

But Kabir drove off leaving his friend puzzled.

After driving for half a kilometre Kabir turned his car and was once again back on the road outside the college. He saw them in front riding on Shakeel's bicycle. The car's powerful headlights showed their position clearly. Mary was holding her lover from behind.

The only emotion ruling Kabir's brain was pure and naked rage. He was ready to unleash all his fury, his vehemence, his humiliation and frustration onto them. Slowly he positioned the car behind them.

Noticing the car's lights, Shakeel moved his cycle to the left but Kabir followed him. Mary turned and saw Kabir. Kabir slammed on the brakes. She waved at him, then replaced her hand on her lover's shoulders.

Kabir paused for a few more seconds, then he put his car into first gear and pressed hard on the accelerator. The powerful car gained speed rapidly and crashed into the bicycle. Both the riders flew in the air before crashing onto the road. The cycle got caught in the car's bumper and was dragged with it as Kabir slammed on the brakes. He got out staggering to where the couple lay just a few feet separating them. Mary's head was in a pool of blood and her eyes were open. She had been killed instantly. Shakeel's head was also bleeding. His eyes were closed and he was breathing loudly. Kabir stood over him and shouted, 'I am Kabir Sabarwal. This is what you get for betraying me.' He hurled abuse after abuse on the unconscious boy. He felt a person catching hold of him from the back. Freeing himself Kabir recognised Rajesh Pahwa.

'Control yourself. No one else is around. I'll drive. Hurry up!' said the student leader pulling Kabir into the car.

Nine

Even four months after the murders of Shakeel and Mary, Kabir felt no remorse over his misdeed. They had betrayed him and had been punished accordingly. Not once did he think that Shakeel had any idea of his feelings for Mary. In fact, he now had delusions that God had shown him the path that his life had to follow. He had become more religious and visited the Temple everyday. He also constantly remembered that he was in the debt of Rajesh Pahwa, now his closest friend.

Kabir still remembered everything vividly. Pahwa's presence of mind and crisis management skills had saved Kabir on that fateful night. Pahwa had first disentangled the cycle from the car's bumper and then driven it straight to the house of one of his co-activists in Karol Bagh. There he had forced Kabir to vomit and have a bath. Kabir was given a fresh set of clothing as he had bloodstains on his trousers and liquor stains on his shirt. Pahwa himself polished Kabir's shoes to remove all traces of blood. The activist and his servant had carefully washed the front of the Chevrolet to remove bloodstains. Just a small dent on the bumper remained, as it couldn't be corrected at that time.

One and a half hours after the murders Kabir was looking fresh but he was frightened and tears would start flowing from his eyes frequently. His mind was getting clearer as the vomiting and the bath removed the effect of alcohol.

Pahwa had made a couple of telephone calls and announced, 'I called the Bara Hindu Rao Hospital. The muslim died before reaching it. People have started gathering there and we should also join them.'

Tears once again flowed freely from Kabir's eyes.

'Don't cry here. Save your tears till we can reach the hospital,' Pahwa had said.

In the hospital, over a hundred people had gathered. The bereaved families were wailing at the death of their young ones.

Pahwa ordered Kabir to join in their sorrow. The police had declared it a hit and run accident because they had no reason to suspect anything else.

Khem Chand, Lajo and Shahida also felt very sorry for Kabir's loss of his best friend. Nobody asked him where he had been the whole day. Kabir told his father that he had probably lost his purse and watch at the hospital and Khem Chand accepted the explanation.

A couple of days earlier, Khem Chand had advised his son, 'I know Shakeel was your best friend. But you need to break out of your sorrow. Make some new friends, go out more.' Kabir sensed an opportunity and asked for permission to invite Rajesh Pahwa to dinner. Khem Chand agreed not knowing that Pahwa had been after his son for this invitation.

Despite his young age, Rajesh Pahwa was a crafty politician ingrained in the Swatantra Sangh's art of deception. He knew how to behave in front of Khem Chand. Entering the bungalow, he first touched the feet of Khem Chand and Lajo. Throughout dinner, he constantly praised the Lala. The topic soon shifted to politics. Knowing Khem Chand's political ideology, Pahwa refused to be drawn into an argument accepting whatever the industrialist said. Lala Khem Chand too hadn't been born yesterday and commented, 'If you agree so much with my views, then why are you an active worker of the I.L.S.?'

'I love and respect my father,' Pahwa carefully replied. 'The Partition really shook him up and he became active in the S.S. It was his desire that I join the student's wing and I can't leave it without disobeying his orders.'

'Then you'll keep working with these fanatics throughout your life,' said Khem Chand.

'Politics is not the aim of my life. My ultimate ambition is to open a big school,' said Pahwa.

The Lala obviously became satisfied with Pahwa's last remarks. He said, 'I am very happy to hear that. When you decide to open that school you come to me. I will be the first to give you a large donation.'

Both friends were very pleased about the successful dinner. It had gone as planned and Rajesh had been accepted by Khem

Chand despite his S.S. credentials. In the past four months, Pahwa's words and his own experiences had greatly affected Kabir. He had lost his tolerance for other religions and stopped visiting the Masjid. As they discussed Kabir's political training, Rajesh decided it was time his friend attended his first political meeting. It was a public meeting of the I.L.S. in Trans Yamuna.

'I'd be happy to attend but what if my photograph appears in the newspaper. These days you are getting a lot of coverage,' said Kabir.

Do not worry. You will not be invited to the stage. You can sit amongst the workers and listen,' replied Rajesh.

Kabir was impressed by his first political meeting. The sloganeering excited him and he listened to each speech carefully. When Rajesh Pahwa's name was announced, the crowd of around a thousand people cheered loudly. The Pahwa name was obviously very popular among them. Rajesh didn't let down that name and gave a rousing speech urging the youth to join and strengthen the I.L.S.

After the meeting, Kabir commented on how Pahwa had received a better ovation than the members of Parliament and senior leaders present. Smiling at Kabir, Pahwa explained, 'My father was one of the founder members of the S.S. thirty years ago. In Lahore he build the organisation from the grassroots level to the top. After Partition he continued working, helping in the rehabilitation of refugees. People respect him as he has never taken any post in the I.L.S. and never contested any election.'

'But we went to a meeting of the I.L.S. Your father is not its member. He has been active only in the S.S.,' said Kabir.

'You still have a lot to learn,' said Pahwa, 'and when your training is complete you will know the answer to your question.'

*

S N Pahwa was having lunch with K K Mishra, propagator-in-chief of the Swatantra Sangh. All in the higher echelons of the organisation were expected to follow a strict code and both of them were firm believers of that code. They were sitting on small mats, food was served on a *patal,* a plate made from large dried leaves. The food was strictly vegetarian. Even the use of onions and garlic wasn't permitted.

During the meal they discussed the upcoming elections. The Indian Lok Sangh was sure to win in Delhi and Gujarat and improve its position elsewhere. Mishra was number two in the S.S. hierarchy. The S.S. Chief, K B Patel stayed at his headquarter in Thane near Bombay. Mishra represented Patel in Delhi and also co-ordinated with the I.L.S., the political wing of the S.S.

S N Pahwa was the chairman of the top secret *Matdaan* wing of the S.S. Literally speaking, *Matdaan* meant votes. But Pahwa's work went well beyond that. During elections, his wing activated the force of the S.S. cadre in every district to poll bogus votes. On election day they formed groups which visited each polling station and cast their votes. The votes, which were cast, were of those people who were out of town, unlikely to vote or people who had expired. Pahwa had successfully demonstrated this technique in a by-election.

The S.S. had most of its thirty lac members in North and Western India. The *Matdaan* wing was fully formed in Delhi and Gujarat to ensure victory in the elections.

'The success or failure of your wing will determine your son's future,' said Mishra.

'Mishra *ji*, my technique cannot be duplicated. Most of the parties do not have a dedicated cadre like the S.S. One day, my idea will make us capture power at the centre,' said Pahwa.

Mishra smiled at his colleague, 'How is your son?' he asked.

'He is very smart and has just be friended Kabir Sabarwal, the sole inheritor of Kabir and Co.'

'But isn't Khem Chand Sabarwal a Congress supporter?'

'Yes, he is. But the boy wants to join us. He is totally under the influence of my son,' said Pahwa proudly.

Ten

As expected, the Indian Lok Sangh pulled off impressive victories in Delhi and Gujarat. For the first time since its inception, the S.S. family now controlled two important states. While the media gave credit to the I.L.S. leadership, the real architects were S.S. leaders like Mishra and S N Pahwa.

The *Matdaan* wing's success had even exceeded Pahwa's own expectations. The old man in Thane, K B Patel, also acknowledged that. When the two incumbent Chief Ministers came to seek his blessings, Patel told them, 'The *Matdaan* wing has done a great job. You both have to honour any request made by them.'

Everyone in the I.L.S. now knew that S N Pahwa had emerged as a strong force in the S.S. and consequently his power had increased manifold. Pahwa himself didn't wish for any political post. His political ambitions were all for his twenty-four-year-old son. A few weeks after the elections, he visited Thane. His association with Patel was thirty years old and they had a comfortable working relationship.

Pahwa wanted his son to be the new head of the youth wing of the I.L.S.

'But before that I want him to train as S.S. propagator here in Thane.'

Patel had expected this request and agreed to it.

'Accompanying him will be Kabir Sabarwal, the heir to Kabir and Co. The boy wants to become a member and I think we should accept him,' Pahwa added.

'We should catch them young so that they are of use to us later. Mishra told me about him, he too can train here,' said Patel.

*

'If I ask him, I'll be grounded for a year. My father will never agree,' said Kabir.

'I have planned it all,' explained Rajesh. 'You have just finished your exams. Tell him you want to holiday in Bombay and Goa for a couple of weeks.'

'I have never gone on a holiday without my family. Daddy won't give me permission.'

'Use your softhearted stepmother. She craves for your love and attention. Be sweet to her and your father will agree,' advised Rajesh.

Rajesh Pahwa was once again proved correct. Lajo convinced Khem Chand and Kabir was granted permission.

Holding the suitcase in his left hand, Kabir paid the taxi driver. The sign over the big doors read 'Swatantra Sangathan National Headquarters.' A couple of burly men in the traditional S.S. dress guarded the door with big *lathis* in their hands. Rajesh approached them and told them who they were. He was given the direction to the main building by one of the guards while the other opened the doors just enough to let them both in.

The size of all he saw greatly impressed Kabir. A ground, the size of two football fields was in the centre, on its three sides were long four-storeyed buildings painted light orange. The S.S. saffron flag was flying in the centre of the ground. All the men they saw walked confidently, chest out, shoulders held high. Kabir noticed them greeting each other with a kind of salute holding their hand in front of them slightly above shoulder level fingers pointing outwards. The two friends were the only ones around who were not wearing the S.S. uniform of khaki shirt and trousers with a black cap.

They entered the main building. Rajesh led the way into a big office. The office was that of the Trainer-in-Chief. He was a tiny fair complexioned man of fifty-five, completely bald. He wore heavy spectacles on his small nose. The plate on his desk read J N Mathur. Rajesh introduced himself and the trainer motioned both of them to sit in the chairs around his desk. He handed them a couple of small books.

'Your training will begin tomorrow. You should be ready and at the assembly by five a.m.,' said Mathur and rang a bell. A young man entered the office and the trainees followed him out.

They were taken to a long dormitory. About twenty cots were lined on either side. Most of them were occupied. Rajesh and Kabir set down their suitcases near two adjacent empty cots. They were both handed big khaki bags. Inside them were two S.S. uniforms, a small soap and a bundle of neem twigs to be used for cleaning teeth.

'I don't need all this stuff. I have a soap and a toothbrush in my bag,' said Kabir.

'We have to follow the system of this place. So we will use whatever they give us,' said Rajesh.

Dinner was a simple affair. All the trainees had to sit cross-legged on the floor and were served a watery dal with rice on a *patal*. No spoons were provided. Kabir hesitated but seeing Rajesh eat with his hands, he followed his friend's actions.

Kabir had trouble sleeping on the coarse cot. He was used to sleeping on a big bed with a soft mattress. The loud snores of his fellow trainees also disturbed him. Finally, his tiredness got the better of him and he fell asleep.

Kabir was woken up by Rajesh. Quickly they had their baths and were ready. Soon they were lined up along with fifty others in the centre of the ground singing religious songs. Two men also in S.S. uniform were in front of them. One of them was Mathur and the other was a tall slim man with blunt features. 'I am Sunil Kumar, your physical trainer,' he introduced himself. As he spoke, Kabir looked around him. The other boys had a look of pride and excitement on their faces. The previous night, at dinner, he had come to know that most of them were high caste Marathis. Several were from Uttar Pradesh and a couple from South India. The S.S. was expanding its base.

Sunil Kumar explained what their training constituted. The boys would be taught gymnastics and *lathi* fighting.

'You will learn to defend Hinduism from the Muslims and attack if called upon by the S.S. Once in a while, you will be allowed to indulge in Indian sports like Kabaddi. Now you will take five laps of this ground and then do twenty push-ups. After that, I'll teach you how to handle a l*athi,'* said Sunil Kumar.

'Remember you are here to learn the traditional Hindu way of life. Speaking in any foreign language will lead to immediate expulsion,' warned Mathur.

While most of the trainees enjoyed the physical training, Rajesh and Kabir hated it. They were not used to physical exertion and eagerly awaited the ideological training sessions. They learnt of the S.S.'s inception, its founders, its massive membership and most importantly, its ideology. Kabir was amazed by all that he learnt. The S.S. had thirty-two lac members. It had thirty-nine subsidiary organisations on its own with branch offices in India and abroad. These organisations controlled trade unions, trader associations, chambers of commerce, social clubs and thousands of temples. They also ran three hundred schools and six hospitals. The S.S. had huge *dharamshalas* in every major Indian city and religious centres. At the bottom of the S.S. structure was its most important part. Weekly *Shakha* meetings were held in every village, town and city of the country. At these meetings the party's ideology and future programmes were discussed. Every night Kabir and Rajesh discussed all that they learnt that day.

'This huge complex and unrestricted expansion couldn't have been possible without the help of the British. After all the S.S.'s growth rate was higher before Independence,' commented Kabir.

'Why state the obvious?' said Rajesh.

On another night Kabir asked his friend about the source of S.S.'s funding.

'There are lacs of rich Hindus in India. They contribute to our cause regularly. In fact, the traders are the backbone of the S.S. family and we too help them out in their needs,' replied Rajesh.

Kabir was also surprised at how the S.S.'s conceptualisation was different from the text books he had been taught from in school and college. The heroes of the S.S. were defenders of the Hindu religion and the Congress's freedom fighters were either looked down upon or not mentioned. The Father of the Nation was considered as having been pro-minorities. They supported the two-nation theory in the sense that all Muslims should be in Pakistan. But for Gandhi *ji*, all the Muslims would have immigrated to Pakistan and the country would be a Hindu state, the S.S. handbook read.

The lectures during the training were repetitive in one sense.

The trainees were constantly reminded that all Muslims were invaders who had looted the country and then stayed back. 'They shouldn't have the right to vote, own property or be elected to any assembly or the Parliament. There should also be a limit on the number of children they bear so that their numbers are kept in check and they cannot ever exceed us in population. Remember we are always in danger and have to protect our faith,' lectured Mathur.

In the last two days of the training they were taught the art of deception. Mathur instructed them, 'The I.L.S. is our political wing. We control all its activities from here. But you should never state this publicly as the I.L.S. is a national party and being remote controlled by a social organisation like ours will discredit its reputation. Never ask for donation or help in the name of the S.S. Always invoke the Hindu God, which that person believes in and he will respond favourably to your request. Never say that you are a Hindu protecting your religion. Always say that you are working to protect Indian traditions and beliefs. Call yourself a true nationalist. Never use the S.S. salute in public. Those who choose to join active politics through the I.L.S. should never publicly declare their support to the S.S. unless asked to do so.'

Mathur ended the ideological training with an order, 'The chief of the S.S. is now your Guru, your link between God and yourself. Always listen to his and only his command from Thane because his word is the word of God. God has chosen the S.S. to represent Him and you are lucky to be a part of His organisation.'

The fourteenth day of the training was one of rejoicing. There was no physical or ideological training. The food served was also a lot better than what had been served before. The trainers and staff were also much more friendly and intermingled with the boys in the lunch time.

In the evening, they were all taken to a hall in one of the buildings. Huge portraits of S.S. heroes hung on the walls and in the centre sat their chief K B Patel. Forming a single line, one by one, they touched his feet and seeked his blessings. 'Welcome to our family,' Patel told every boy.

Rajesh was ahead of Kabir and when he touched the Chief's feet, Mathur whispered something in the old man's ear. Patel smiled first at Rajesh and then looked at Kabir.

'You have both done well. Welcome to our family,' he said.

Eleven

Kabir's changed personality worried his father. Physically, Kabir had become leaner and slightly taller. He now walked like an army man, shoulders held high and chest out. Khem Chand had loved his son's quiet intelligence but since his holiday, Kabir had become brash and arrogant. He bossed over the servants constantly scolding them. He had once again become cold towards Lajo. With the Lala he was still respectful but tried to avoid eye contact, like he was hiding something important.

Khem Chand knew that Kabir was not telling the truth about his holiday. Kabir's narrative about the holiday seemed like a well-rehearsed speech rather than a young man's account of his first holiday with friends. Khem Chand talked to Lajo about his doubts.

'He probably holidayed with some girl and wants to avoid telling you about it. He is no longer a child and deserves to be treated like an adult,' Lajo said. Khem Chand accepted his wife's reasoning but continued to worry. He knew that Kabir's only companion on the trip had been Rajesh Pahwa. 'Pahwa's influence on my son has to be curtailed in the future,' he thought.

Shahida Bibi was also very troubled by Kabir's changed behaviour. He had become totally indifferent towards her, sometimes not speaking to her for several days. It was as if she no longer existed for him. After a month of this treatment, she decided to talk to him.

'What is wrong, son? You don't speak to me any more,' she said tousling his hair.

Kabir roughly removed her hand from his hair. 'There is nothing wrong. These days I am very busy,' he said.

'But you don't come with me to the Mosque. Have I done something wrong?' asked the old woman.

Kabir raised his voice, 'I don't want to go to your Mosque. I am a Hindu, why should I go there?'

'Your father named you Kabir. He wants you to respect all religions and you...'

Kabir interrupted her, 'My name and the matters about which you speak, are affairs between my father and myself. You have no business to interfere.'

'I have raised you like my own son. Now after twenty years you tell me it's none of my business. My nephew always writes to me calling me to Lucknow. But I always refuse because of my love for you,' said Shahida her eyes filling with tears.

'You should go to Lucknow, nobody needs you here. And as for raising me up, you were always paid for your services,' said Kabir. 'You are lucky my father gave you a job.'

Tears were now flowing freely from her eyes. 'I will leave, my son and never come back.'

'You should leave. Don't call me son. My mother was killed by your people. You Muslims should all be kicked out of here to Pakistan,' Kabir said vehemently and left the room.

Shahida's decision to leave saddened Khem Chand. She had become a part of the Sabarwal family. The Lala looked upon her as a sister and had never considered her a servant. He requested her not to leave and asked her if Kabir had done something causing her taking this sudden a decision.

'No, Lala *ji,* Kabir is now grown up. I have done my duty to the best of my ability. My nephew has two small children and his wife doesn't keep well. I have to help him,' said Shahida. Lajo too requested her not to leave but Shahida was adamant.

Khem Chand summoned his son, 'Shahida is leaving us after all these years. Have you said or done anything to offend her?'

'No, it seems she wants to help her nephew,' replied Kabir.

Khem Chand personally drove Shahida to the railway station, accompanied by Lajo and Kabir. As she got on the train, Lajo handed her a packet of money and a bag full of gifts.

'I do not need this, Lala *ji*. The respect you have given me all these years is enough for me,' said Shahida.

Tears filled Khem Chand's eyes, 'These gifts are for your nephew and his family. You are my sister and never forget that,' he said emotionally.

'Thank you, Lala *ji.*'

'No, Shahida. It is I who should be thankful to you. You have made my son grow to this age.'

He motioned Kabir to touch her feet. Knowing that any refusal would arouse suspicion, Kabir quickly touched Shahida's feet. She smiled despite her tears and blessed him. 'May *Allah* show you the right path. May you always prosper in life.'

As the train left the platform, Khem Chand kept staring it.

'What is this?' asked Kabir holding a packet. It was the packet of money Lajo had given to Shahida.

'Where did this come from?' asked Lajo.

'It was in my coat pocket,' said Kabir, 'Who put it there?'

'Son, the proud lady has passed on the money we gave her, to you. You are lucky that you have been raised by such a great human being,' said the Lala.

*

'You have committed a grave error. Don't you remember what we were taught in Thane?' said Rajesh Pahwa. 'Those who are not in active politics do not have to show their true feelings till absolutely necessary. We are lucky the old hag didn't tell your father about your feelings. If she had, our association would have to end.'

They were alone in Pahwa's new office in the I.L.S. headquarters.

'I am sorry about it. I'll be careful in the future,' said Kabir sullenly.

Rajesh smiled at his friend. 'How do you like the decor of my office?' he asked changing the topic.

'It is nice but what use is it? You are hardly here,' said Kabir.

What Kabir said was true. Ever since he became the All India President of the youth wing of the I.L.S., Pahwa hardly stayed in Delhi. He was always on tour visiting different states, addressing meetings and building the organisation. A horde of local I.L.S. youth activists followed Rajesh whenever he was back in Delhi. This irked Kabir as the two friends were never alone even to discuss important matters.

'I know you don't like all these hangers-on,' said Rajesh. 'But I know you like some of the girls who are among them.'

'I haven't even noticed any of them,' said Kabir.

'One of them seems to like you a lot. She keeps asking about you, your likes and dislikes. She even enquired whether you have a girlfriend or not.'

'I am not interested. But who is she anyway?' asked Kabir.

Pahwa smiled, 'Her name is Taruna Singh. She is the tall, fair and buxom one with fine features. We studied at the same college, she was a year junior to me.'

'That means she is three years older to me.'

'Remember, if she is older it means that she is experienced. I have set a dinner date for you. Enjoy yourself.'

Taruna Singh was born and brought up in a small town in central Uttar Pradesh. Her father was the principal of a S. S. run school and used his contacts to get her admitted into a college in Delhi. At a political meeting in her college she had noticed Rajesh Pahwa. Even then Pahwa was respected by all activists for his background, oratorical skills and political intelligence. As there was a dearth of female political activists, Pahwa promoted her career. Very soon, they became lovers.

Taruna became a powerful activist of Delhi University and was noticed by the top brass of the I.L.S. One day, Pahwa received a call from the National General Secretary of the I.L.S. Without any pretensions he ordered Pahwa to send Taruna to his house as he wanted to spend the night with her.

He added that if she agreed she would be immediately rewarded with an important political post and her future would be looked after by him. Rajesh and Taruna discussed the demand for an hour. They both knew that the General Secretary would surely harm their future if they didn't obey him. Finally, she agreed.

In the last few years, she had risen politically and had gone to bed with several I.L.S. leaders. Her liaison with Pahwa had also continued. In fact, it was he who had asked her to start a relationship with Kabir. 'He is inexperienced and awkward in front of girls. Because of you, he will become confident and experienced.'

Dining at the Swanky Restaurant, Kabir felt uncomfortable in front of the more experienced girl. They talked very little and quickly finished their meal. As Kabir stopped the car in front of Taruna's small house, she looked deeply into his eyes. 'You have beautiful eyes,' she said softly and kissed him on the cheek. Her move caused Kabir to freeze and he sat still. She took his face in her hands and gave him a deep kiss on his lips. 'Come in. I live alone,' she said taking his hand.

His relationship with Taruna completely took over Kabir's mind. Her thoughts filled his brain. Throughout the day, he awaited their meeting every evening. After he came home he vividly went over all that transpired when they were together Taruna's magnificent body and experience was becoming an obsession for him. They had continuous, pure, animal sex whenever they were together. Kabir couldn't keep his hands off her even when they were in public places like restaurants.

One day, Pahwa opened his office to find them locked in a passionate embrace. 'It has been three months since you have done any party work,' he scolded Taruna in front of her lover. 'The party President wants you to immediately leave for Bihar. Go meet him in his office.' Taruna quickly left the room. Turning to Kabir, he said, 'I know you are crazy about her. Love her physically and just physically. Enjoy her but don't fall in love. Enjoy all the fish around, now that you are experienced.'

Taruna stayed in Bihar for two months. By the time she returned to Delhi, Kabir had a new seventeen-year old girl friend. Pahwa was proud that his friend had learned so fast.

Twelve

Kabir's twenty-first birthday party was a grand affair. Coloured lights adorned the bungalow's walls and trees. A huge sign of lights atop the terrace read '21'. Khem Chand had invited Delhi's leading personalities and over five hundred guests attended. The Lala and Lajo intermingled with the guests and played the perfect hosts. Kabir along with Pahwa and several friends stood in a corner of the lawn. He respectfully thanked the guests who wished him but had a nonchalant attitude about the party. Thrice the Lala told his son to be at his side but as soon his father's back turned, Kabir returned to his friends. Kabir had just graduated and was ready to start working with his father. It was because of this reason that Khem Chand wanted him to meet the important guests. But Kabir spent almost the entire evening in the company of his friends.

That night in their bedroom Khem Chand and Lajo talked about the party. 'Kabir's indifference has become intolerable. He disobeys me constantly. I told him several times to stay at my side but he would disappear after a few minutes. Pahwa has completely spoilt him,' said the worried father.

'He has just finished college. After few years, he will forget his friends,' said Lajo.

'I wanted him to go abroad for further studies but he refused outright. Kabir and Co. is now among India's top twenty industrial houses and a foreign degree would have benefited his future in it.'

'Look at the brighter side. He will learn the business at a younger age. I think you should send him to see all our units throughout India,' advised Lajo.

'That is an excellent idea. A tour of all our factories and offices will take at least six months. He will slip out of Pahwa's grip by then,' said the Lala.

'I am glad you like my idea,' said Lajo.

'Don't you regret your decision not to have any children?' asked Khem Chand.

'I have a son named Kabir. Why should I regret my decision?' said Lajo.

A fortnight after his twenty-first birthday, Kabir was appointed as a director in Kabir and Co. His first responsibility was surveying the group's units and offices all over India.

Khem Chand personally planned his son's itinerary. Starting from Tamil Nadu, Kabir would visit all the twenty-two manufacturing units and seven major regional offices of the group. Two executives would accompany him wherever he went. He had to spend at least five days understanding the working of the particular unit or office.

Kabir started the tour with a sullen and disinterested attitude. But as it progressed, his curiosity and interest in the business grew day by day. The incredible wealth of Kabir and Co. amazed the young man. He began to respect his father's business acumen and vision for the future. In little more than twenty years the group was the country's largest manufacturer of steel pipes, sugar, heavy chemicals and fertilisers. It was among the top ten producers of tyres, home appliances and photographic equipments.

The conglomerate was also one of the biggest real estate owner in the country. None of its subsidiaries ever rented a factory or an office. Real estate was always purchased albeit with a heavy investment. The debt equity ratio of the group was the lowest among the top twenty business houses. This greatly enhanced its ability to survive any slow-down in the economy and gave it leverage to expand in the future.

Kabir's fascination for his conglomerate increased when he thought of the great power source it constituted. 'One day, I will use this power to become the most powerful man in India,' he thought.

Throughout his tour he corresponded regularly with Rajesh. They both knew that the tour was being used by Khem Chand to separate them and took care that he should not succeed.

Khem Chand monitored his son's tour and got a pleasant surprise when he received suggestions from him on how to improve the working of some of the units. Though most of the suggestions displayed Kabir's naivety, a few impressed even Sanjeev Khanna, now the Chief Executive of the entire group.

The tour kept him away from home for seven months. During this period, every single manager of Kabir and Co. had personally met him. He had also come to understand the nitty gritty of every unit owned by the group.

On his return home, Khem Chand held a small dinner inviting the top managers of his head office. During dinner Kabir sensed a change in his father's attitude towards him. Khem Chand no longer treated him like a young boy and addressed him with respect. Driving back from dinner, father and son were seated in the back seat of the Mercedes, when Khem Chand patted his son on the back and tousled his hair.

'In the next few years I will retire. I am growing old and want to spend a quiet peaceful life with your mother. I have built this empire on one and only one policy and that is generation of wealth for welfare. Not only our welfare but the welfare of our employees, dealers, customers and even that of the small tea stall owners outside our big factories. Remember this *Mantra* and you will always succeed and our empire will continue to grow.'

Kabir nodded his head and said, 'I will always remember it.'

The next day at breakfast Kabir noticed his father and Lajo constantly exchanging glances. 'I feel you both want to say something to me,' he said. Lajo looked at her husband and then said, 'Your father and I have decided that it is time for you to marry. We have found a suitable girl for you. She is the daughter of Sardar Gurnam Singh and is extremely beautiful. We both want you to see her as soon as possible,' Lajo's words shocked Kabir. He was totally unprepared for this and didn't know how to react.

'I am too young to be married,' he said leaving the table.

'Where are you going?' asked Khem Chand.

'I have to meet a friend,' Kabir replied.

★

'This matter was bound to crop up. I agree with your parents. It is time you got married,' said Rajesh Pahwa swivelling his chair.

'You are the limit. You are older than me. Why don't you get married?' said Kabir.

Rajesh laughed and said, 'I am not the sole heir to the Sabarwal wealth.'

'You want me to marry a Sikh girl and you call yourself a defender of the Hindu faith,' said Kabir indignantly.

'I didn't say you should marry a Sikh girl. I just said it is the right time for you to marry. You cannot fight your parents on this issue. As for the girl, I promise I'll find you a pure Hindu bride,' said Rajesh.

Rajesh discussed Kabir's problem with his father. 'The employees of the Sabarwal household can be useful in this regard. Some of your youth workers should meet them and tell them about the Sikh girl's bad reputation. One of your workers should meet the Lala and say that he is a lover of the girl and they planned to get married. This will create a doubt in Khem Chand's mind,' advised the senior Pahwa.

'But we will have to find a suitable girl for Kabir,' said Rajesh.

'Madan Mohan Sahni's elder daughter is eligible for marriage. Tomorrow, I will speak to him,' his father replied.

Thirteen

Before Partition, Madam Mohan Sahni managed his father's tiny jewellery shop in Lahore. Being an active worker of the S.S., he regularly attended its *Shakha* meetings. In July 1947, while he was getting married in Jammu, Lahore, his house and shop were completely destroyed. A self respecting man, he refused to stay at his in-law's house and moved to a relative's village near Ludhiana. Leaving his elderly parents and new bride, Sahni arrived in Delhi.

The twenty-two year old spent a futile couple of months looking for work. In desperation, he began peddling combs and mirrors on the pavements of Connaught Place. One day, while selling his ware he came to know from a customer that the Swatantra Sangh was holding a meeting for all its activists from West Punjab. The S.S. wanted to reactivate its dispersed activists.

At the meeting, Sahni met S N Pahwa. He had worked under Pahwa in Lahore and had a great respect for him. Pahwa liked the young man and saw a future for him in the S.S. He offered Sahni an important post in the Delhi unit of S.S. The young man politely declined the offer, 'Pahwa *ji*, my elderly parents and wife are in Ludhiana. I came to Delhi hoping to find a suitable job. Now I sell combs and mirrors on the footpath. I don't need a political post. What I need is some work so that I can sustain my family.' The S.S. needed an intelligent man to co-ordinate with the newly set up Rehabilitation Ministry. Pahwa had been asked to find such a man and he offered the job to Sahni. 'You will get a small commission for every claim that is settled. But before that you have to build relations with the staff at the Ministry.' Sahni accepted the offer without hesitation.

Street smart and a consummate hustler, Sahni soon build relations with almost the entire staff of the Ministry. He was soon friendly with all the concerned peons and clerks and even a couple of top bureaucrats. The S.S. sent him many refugees and within a year Sahni's savings from his commissions amounted to twenty thousand rupees. It was then that he embarked on his more profitable routine.

Through his relatives in Ludhiana and Jammu, he got numerous requests from refugees. These refugees couldn't travel to Delhi and were totally dependent on him. Sahni started buying their claims, as most of them were a desperate lot willing to sell their claims for a pittance. He bought claims for as low as twenty per cent of the settled value. In a few months Sahni was so successful that he had to borrow to finance his purchases.

Four years after Partition, Sahni was worth several lacs. He left Delhi to return to settle in Ludhiana. He started trading in gold jewellery, setting up big shops in all the major towns of Punjab. Using his contacts in the S.S., he also started buying large tracts of agricultural land.

By 1970, Madan Mohan Sahni was one of the wealthiest men in Punjab. He owned a chain of jewellery shops, four flour mills, a rice mill and thousands of acres of agricultural land. A consistent contributor to the S.S., he was connected with Deshmukh in Thane and several other top I.L.S. leaders. His relation with Pahwa had continued and he still respected him as before. At forty-five his sole aim in life was finding suitable husbands for his two daughters.

Pahwa's enquiry about his older daughter Radhika, overjoyed Sahni. He understood Pahwa's orders. Khem Chand would have to be contacted by an intermediatory who had no known links with the S.S.

Sahni knew the right man for the job. Davinder Chatrath was a small industrialist of Ludhiana, manufacturing rubber chemicals used by Kabir Tyres. Chatrath knew the Lala pretty well. He was very close to Sahni and when contacted, he agreed to talk to Khem Chand.

On receiving the proposal Khem Chand was very pleased. He was on the look out for a suitable daughter-in-law ever since he had come to know about the many love affairs of Gurnam Singh's daughter. Khem Chand had heard about Sahni and his wealth.

Chatrath said, 'Lala *ji,* next Sunday Sahni and his family will be in Delhi. He would like you all to be his guests at his brother-in-law's house.'

'Tell Mr Sahni we will be pleased to be his guests,' replied Khem Chand.

Awaiting the arrival of the Sabarwals, Lata Sahni issued last minute instructions to her elder daughter, Radhika, 'Remember, you are the daughter of a honourable family. Do not speak too much, keep your head bowed and do not raise you eyes.'

'Yes, Mata *ji*', said Radhika.

Five foot three inches in height, extremely fair in complexion, with delicate features and long hair, Radhika was an irresistible beauty. Lata was sure that the Sabarwal family would accept her on sight.

All her life Radhika had never disobeyed her parents. Madan Mohan and Lata had raised her conservatively. She was imbibed in the traditional Hindu culture prescribed by the S.S. Ever since she had attained puberty she had been allowed to wear only salwar kameez dresses. Her mother constantly warned her to keep away from boys, knowing that her daughter's beauty attracted many.

Radhika had been taught from childhood to be a proud and devout Hindu. Every day, she got up at six, bathed and then conducted a hour long *Pooja*. She had studied at a girls school and her schooling had just concluded. Sahni was anxious to get her married. He still remembered the S.S. training, 'A young girl should be married as early as possible.'

As Khem Chand entered the large house on Pusa Road, he was immediately put off by the man who welcomed him. Short, rotund and almost completely bald, Sahni loudly welcomed them.

Soon they were all seated in the plush drawing room. While the men discussed business, Lata Sahni told Lajo about her daughter's many virtues. '*Behan ji*, she is a very homely and shy girl. She loves cooking and doing household chores. She is also very intelligent and topped the merit list in her school.'

'Then why didn't you send her to college?' asked Lajo.

'Sahni *Sahab* is very strict. He wanted her to be married after she finished schooling.'

Khem Chand was getting irritated by Sahni's haughtiness. He was feeling uncomfortable and having second thoughts about the Sahnis. Just then Radhika entered the room in a bright pink

Salwar Kameez carrying a tray laden with tea and snacks.

Looking at her Khem Chand immediately felt that this beautiful petite girl had been born to be his daughter-in-law. Lajo also felt the same and asked Radhika to sit near her. Kabir was pleasantly surprised as he stared at her.

Rajesh had briefed him about the Sahni's and their beautiful daughter. But the girl's beauty surpassed his friend's description.

Madan Mohan and Lata noticed their reactions and triumphantly smiled at each other.

The news of Kabir's engagement with Radhika rapidly spread in the business circles of Delhi. Kabir was one of the most eligible bachelors and many prospective father-in-laws were disappointed.

Ashok Chand Gupta came to know about the engagement from one of his creditors. He remembered the day he had received the report from the International Detective Agency. It had read – 'Kabir Sabarwal is not the biological son of Lala Khem Chand Sabarwal. This information was given to us by one Mahendra Mehta, first cousin of Khem Chand. The Lala had found the infant Kabir in the arms of the boy's dying father. Kabir is the son of a nephew of Sabarwal's manager. The name of the manager was Ishaque Akhtar and his nephew was called Nooruddin Akhtar.

Mr Mehta recalls that Nooruddin was a drunkard until Sabarwal got him a job in the railways. Nooruddin's entire family including his wife were killed in riots in Delhi while they were visiting his in-laws. The infant Kabir was the only survivor and spent three days at the house of a constable of Delhi Police.

'We have enclosed copies of a police report about the death of the Akhtar family. The report also shows that the one-month-old Kabir was handed over to his father an employee in the railways.'

Ashok now had the chance to get back at the Lala. For almost five years he hadn't used the report waiting for an oppurtunate moment. Ashok was in dire straits and this was the right time to blackmail Khem Chand and extort a large sum from him. He picked up the telephone directory and started looking for the Lala's phone number.

Fourteen

Ashok Gupta's request for an appointment perturbed Khem Chand. He knew that in the last few months Ashok had borrowed heavily to invest in real estate. The market had gone down and he was now facing financial ruin. Reluctantly Khem Chand ordered his secretary to adjust Ashok in his busy schedule.

Ashok entered the lift in Kabir and Co's multi-storeyed office building. 'On which floor is Khem Chand's office?' He rudely asked the liftman. 'Twelfth floor,' was the curt reply.

A few minutes later, he was seated in Khem Chand's modest office.

'Our money has been lucky for you,' mocked Ashok.

Khem Chand replied, 'It wasn't your money. It was the hard earned money of your brother. He gave you five times of what he gave me and today you are virtually bankrupt.'

'You are right. I am almost bankrupt but at least I am not a deceitful liar,' said Ashok raising his voice.

'How dare you speak like this? Get out,' said Khem Chand angrily.

'I will go, but before that you read these papers,' he said taking the report out of his pocket.

Not wanting a scene in his office and wanting to get rid of Ashok, Khem Chand accepted the papers. Putting on his glasses, he started reading.

The Lala's hands started shaking as he read the report. After he had finished reading, he silently gazed at it unable to speak.

'I can see that you are no longer angry with me,' said Ashok. Trying to compose himself, Khem Chand asked, 'What is it that you want?'

'The report in front of you is a copy of the original. You can have it but it will cost you.'

'How much?' asked the Lala.

'Twenty-five lakhs in cash by next Monday,' the blackmailer

replied.

'You will be paid on Monday. Now get out of my office,' said Khem Chand.

On the designated day, they were seated in Khem Chand's Mercedes, parked near Pragati Maidan. Khem Chand examined the report finding it to be the original one, he handed over a large briefcase to Ashok.

'You can count the money, if you want to,' he said.

'I know you won't cheat me on this matter,' said Ashok opening the car door.

'Remember one thing. If I ever see your face again, it will be the last day of your life,' warned Khem Chand.

Seeing the vehement expression on the Lala's face, Ashok kept quiet and just nodded his head. Getting into his Ambassador parked on the other side of the road, Ashok carefully placed the suitcase on the front seat next to him. He reached for the whiskey bottle under the seat, he carefully opened the seal and took a large swig.

Ashok drove his car all over New Delhi, drinking continuously. After more than a hour he was completely drunk having consumed the whole bottle. It was dark and he decided to return home. He planned to show off the money to his wife and parents. In the last few months they had all become disrespectful and hostile towards him. 'Now once again they will fear and respect me,' he thought.

In a hurry to return home, Ashok drove faster. As he reached the Mahatma Gandhi Road he changed lanes frequently, overtaking other vehicles. Near Rajghat he overtook a car. As the car gave way, he suddenly saw a stationary truck in front of him, parked alongside the road's divider. Unable to once again change lanes, Ashok slammed hard on the brakes. But the alcohol had slowed down his reflexes and it was too late. The car crashed into the heavy truck. The truck was carrying inflammable chemicals. After just a few seconds, the truck and the car both exploded with an ear-shattering bang.

Four months after their engagement, Kabir and Radhika were married at a lavish ceremony in Ludhiana.

Despite Khem Chand's request for no dowry, Radhika brought a dowry which couldn't be matched by even the biggest Maharaja's in India.

Two days after the wedding, the Lala gave a big reception at Oberoi Hotel. Those who graced the occasion included the Prime Minister and almost her entire Cabinet, Members of Parliament, several important Chief Ministers, representatives of the leading business houses and scores of top ranking bureaucrats. A couple of film stars from Bombay performed in a stage show entertaining the guests.

Khem Chand noticed that most of his guests discussed the influx of refugees from East Pakistan and its affect on Indo-Pak relations. Businessmen pestered the politicians on whether or not we would go to war with Pakistan. Khem Chand didn't want his son and daughter-in-law to travel outside the country in view of the impending war. He had decided that they would have a quiet honeymoon in their farmhouse in the foothills of the Himalayas.

The day after Kabir's reception, Rajesh Pahwa's father woke him up.

'Get ready immediately. We have to be at an emergency meeting called by Mishra *ji*.'

Rajesh quickly got ready. After all, it was the first time he had been asked to attend a meeting convened by the S.S. General Secretary.

On their way to the regional S.S. office in Karol Bagh, he asked his father about the agenda of the meeting. 'We have to decide our course of action on the East Pakistan issue,' replied the Senior Pahwa.

As they entered the large meeting hall, Mishra greeted them curtly. Already seated on the chairs were the eleven members of the I.L.S. National Committee, I.L.S. State Chiefs and several top ranking S.S. functionaries.

After they were all settled, Mishra got up. He saluted them in the traditional S.S. style and started speaking.

'I have information that several million people will cross into our country from East Pakistan. If this situation continues, India will soon be inundated by these Muslim refugees. I also have definite information that Indira Gandhi is contemplating war with

Pakistan. Now we have to decide which course to take. Our *Shakha* meetings have already been propagating stern actions like firing on those who cross the border. The I.L.S. has demanded milder measures like segregation of the refugees in camps.'

'But the feedback from our cadres is different. They want India to immediately attack Pakistan and before that we should be the first to call for war.'

'Yesterday night, I spoke to the old man in Thane and he has left the decision on you people.'

The tall gaunt I.L.S. Vice President, Lalit Shukla got up.

'If there is a war, India will win and in the next general elections, the opposition will surely be swept aside by a massive Congress wave. It is imperative for our political survival that we immediately call for war,' he said.

'Shukla *ji* is right. The I.L.S. is considered a nationalist party and a call for war will reinforce that impression,' said S N Pahwa.

The next speaker was the portly head of the Traders Department of the I.L.S., 'My fellow traders will also support the call for war.'

He was interrupted by Mishra, 'Your moral support is not enough. If there is a war your associates will benefit the most.'

The trader wiped his sweaty forehead and said nervously, 'We will finance all the programmes undertaken in this regard.'

Rajesh quietly sat through the entire meeting. He knew he was considered too young to discuss the issue and had been invited just to listen and learn. Towards the end of the meeting, Mishra instructed him, 'Within a week, I want your youth wing to hold a big demonstration at the Boat Club demanding military action against Pakistan. After that, the parent body will organise a Delhi *bandh* on the issue.'

Fifteen

The Sabarwal farm was two hundred kilometres from Delhi in idyllic Kotdwara, on the foothills of the Himalayas. It was more than hundred acres in size, bordered on three sides by a dense forest. The natural state of the land hadn't been disturbed and tall trees mostly covered it. Only a small part of it was cultivated upon by the three families of local villagers who also managed the entire farm.

A small colonial house was in the centre of the farm. Two years ago, when Khem Chand had bought the farm it had been in a dilapidated condition. Now it had been completely repaired and equipped with modern household amenities. Flowers of all kinds bloomed in the sprawling gardens surrounding the house, enhancing its beauty.

Kabir and Radhika had reservations about spending their honeymoon in Kotdwara. But once they set their eyes upon the colonial house, its garden and the scenic beauty of the hills surrounding it, they loved it.

Radhika's beautiful young body completely obsessed Kabir. The first five days of the honeymoon were spent by him making mad passionate love to her all night and most of the day. Whatever little sleep Kabir got was filled with dreams of her body.

However, towards the end of the week, Kabir's euphoria on having such a beautiful wife was waning. Radhika's sweet, homely nature, greatly appreciated by his parents, had begun to irritate him. She was not the least bit adventurous or outgoing. Kabir had wanted to venture into the forest on foot but she had refused. She was also very superstitious and mumbling *shlokas* almost the entire day. Despite being a brilliant student, Radhika's general knowledge was poor. Kabir suspected that she had passed all her exams by cramming up the subjects rather than understanding them. She also had a small town naiveness and was no match for his superior intellect. This was creating an invisible wall between them even on their honeymoon.

Kabir managed to cajole his wife into a trip to the forest in the farm's jeep. They started early in the morning. A farmer drove the jeep. Kabir asked him, 'Which animals can be seen around here?'

'*Sahab*, there are lots of elephants and deer and if we are lucky, we may sight a tiger or a leopard,' replied the driver.

'Then how will we protect ourselves?' asked Radhika in a frightened voice.

Kabir's exasperation was evident. 'We'll use our bare hands,' he said.

The next day, Kabir was itching to return to Delhi. Newspapers predicted that a war would start any day and he had read about Rajesh Pahwa's successful demonstration demanding an attack on Pakistan. He was also completely bored and getting increasingly impatient with Radhika.

In the jungle she had behaved like a ten-year-old. Squealing with delight on seeing deer and monkeys and screaming with fear when they had come upon a herd of wild elephants.

Contrary to Kabir's expectation, Radhika was not disappointed by his decision to cut short their honeymoon. 'You must be missing Daddy *ji* and Mummy *ji*,' she said.

Kabir was relieved by her acceptance and said, 'Yes, I am missing them.'

'However, there is one thing you must do for me,' requested Radhika.

'What is it?' asked Kabir suspiciously.

'Tomorrow is an auspicious day. We should return via Haridwar so that we can take a dip in the Ganga,' replied Radhika.

Two days after Kabir returned to Delhi, India was at war with Pakistan. Khem Chand immediately called an emergency meeting of Kabir and Co. Ltd.'s board of directors. Sanjeev Khanna had prepared a list of services that the group could provide to help in the war effort. Most of the trucks of the group would be immediately put at the army's disposal. Kabir and Co. would take the lead in contributing to the Prime Minister's Relief Fund. Also, Khem Chand would personally contact other industrialists and request contributions to the fund.

After the board had accepted the proposals unanimously,

Khem Chand got up to speak. 'We have trucks, money and we will do everything possible to help our country in these difficult times. But there are others who need us. Thousands will be displaced from the villages and towns along the borders. The government will do its bit by setting up relief camps but that will not be enough. I feel an affinity with these people because I know how it feels to leave your house and property not knowing whether you will be able to go back or not.

Therefore, I have decided that my wife and I will undertake a tour of these relief camps. With us will be trucks laden with food packets, clothes, blankets, toiletries and other essential items.'

All the directors of Kabir and Co. proudly gave their Chairman a standing ovation.

In the next forty-eight hours, Sanjeev Khanna organised everything. The necessary permissions were taken, a six member staff was to accompany the couple and five trucks were totally filled with the goods ordered by the Lala. The only problem was the Lala himself. He had suddenly fallen sick with high fever and consequently, had to be bedridden for at least a week.

'You can easily defer your journey for a week,' said Kabir. They were all sitting in Khem Chand's bedroom.

'I don't want to postpone. Those poor people need us now,' said Khem Chand.

'The doctor says you need at least a week's rest. You can't possibly go,' said Kabir.

Lajo interjected, 'Lala *ji*, you have to rest. Don't worry about the displaced people, I'll go.'

'Without me?' asked Khem Chand.

Both Kabir and Radhika were surprised by the conviction and firmness in Lajo's voice.

'Yes, I will go without you. I feel it is my duty to help these people and I will do so.'

Khem Chand realised that his wife was adamant and he agreed reluctantly.

Lajo handed over the keys of the entire house to Radhika. 'You are now in charge of the Sabarwal family,' she said. Radhika hugged her mother-in-law emotionally. Lajo touched Kabir's cheeks affectionately, 'Goodbye, son,' was all she said.

Khem Chand had come outside to see her off. Lajo scolded him mildly, 'You never follow my orders. I told you not to come out.'

He said, 'We are being separated for the first time in eight years. How could I stay in my room?' His words touched her.

'I am not going forever. Don't worry so much. I'll keep away from the front,' she reassured him.

Even ten minutes after the convoy had left, Khem Chand stood in the porch praying silently to the idols of Hindu Gods standing in the bungalow's garden. 'Protect her, don't make me lonely again,' he murmured at the end of his prayer.

Sixteen

Shrill air raid sirens disturbed the tranquillity of the night as Kabir returned home from the office. The servants were busy switching off the lights when he entered the house. A servant with a candle showed the way to his room. Radhika served dinner in their bedroom while he changed. Just as they were about to start eating, there was loud knock on the door.

'Who is it?' said Kabir angrily.

A servant entered. 'One *Sahab* has come to meet you.'

'Who is it, disturbing us at this unearthly hour?'

'It is a *Sahab* in a military uniform,' replied the servant.

'Tell him I am coming,' said Kabir slipping on an overcoat over his night suit. .

He carefully descended the dimly lit stairs recognising the unexpected visitor. It was Brigadier Surindra Singh. He was stationed at Army headquarters and a good friend of Khem Chand. They quietly greeted each other. Brigadier Singh wasn't his usual boisterous self and knowing something was bothering him, Kabir asked him the purpose of his late night visit.

'You have to keep a big heart, one cannot fight fate,' said Singh.

'What is the matter? Tell me directly,' demanded Kabir getting panicky.

'Son, it is about your mother. Today, she was travelling on the highway near Jammu. Thinking the convoy to be a military one, a Pakistani plane bombed it. There were no survivors, I am very sorry.'

In spite of his cold relationship with his stepmother, the tragic news made Kabir cry.

The Brigadier tapped his shoulders, 'We have to inform Lala *ji.*'

When Khem Chand saw Kabir and Singh enter his room, he realised something serious and happened. 'Is Lajo all right?' he asked Singh.

Singh replied gravely, 'I am afraid not Lala *ji*. She was killed today.'

Kabir could see the effect the news had on his father. Khem Chand's broad shoulders slumped and his hands began trembling. Holding the bedpost for support, he slowly sat on the bed. Tears flowing freely from his eyes, in a shaky voice he told Kabir, 'You call up Sanjeev. He will inform everyone and look after the funeral arrangements.'

Turning to the Brigadier he said, 'Thank you for informing me personally. When will we have her body?'

'Early tomorrow morning,' replied Singh.

Lajo's last rites were performed at the Nigambodh Ghat on the banks of the Yamuna River. In spite of the ongoing war hundreds assembled to pay their last respects. The Lala slowly and carefully completed the rites. For the first time in his life, he looked his age. Dark circles under his eyes seemed to enhance the wrinkles on his face. His whole frame had drooped and he trembled as he slowly got up to light the funeral pyre.

As the flames consumed Lajo's body, he was reminded of the ghastly deaths of his first wife and sons and how he had cremated their bodies.

After the formalities were completed, Khem Chand, Kabir and Madan Mohan Sahni stood at the exit of the cremation area with folded hands. This was the customary way of receiving the condolences of the people who had come for the cremation. After the last man walked by, Kabir looked at his father. The Lala's eyes were half-closed and he was leaning against the wall, his hands were still folded.

'Daddy it is time to leave,' he said.

Taking his father's arm Kabir led him towards the parking area. They had walked for a few feet when all of a sudden Khem Chand collapsed.

The Lala convalesced slowly from his first heart attack. After a week at the hospital his doctor ordered another eight weeks of complete bed rest. At home, he was looked after by his dutiful daughter-in-law and a nurse hired specifically for him.

Khem Chand's prolonged illness presented an opportunity for

Kabir to expand his influence in Kabir and Co. He consulted Rajesh Pahwa. 'You have to change the important managers in your group. The present ones will never respect you. For them you always will be the son of the Lala. But you can't do so right away. First, you must hire new people and train them, so that they can one day take over from the present lot.' Pahwa had advised him.

Kabir moved quickly. He hired several new executives giving them a supervisory role over key group subsidiaries. They were answerable only to Kabir and were instructed not to report to any other director.

India had won the war and Kabir was readying the group to grab the new business opportunities likely to crop up. However, most of his decisions brought him at loggerhead with Sanjeev Khanna. Sanjeev barged into his office and confronted him, 'Your decision on the recently hired managers having supervisory powers over key group companies does not have the board's sanction.'

'My father and I own ninety per cent of Kabir and Co., which in turns owns fifty-one per cent of all its subsidiaries. That means I can overthrow the board whenever I wish to,' said Kabir, 'As for the duties of the new managers, they are in their present capacities only for a short period and will be shifted elsewhere after a few months.'

'What about your decision to go into grains trading? You have authorised construction of huge storage facilities. An eight member staff team is surveying the market. You should know that this kind of business is not suitable for a conglomerate of our size. Most of the deals are in the grey market, black money is freely used,' said Sanjeev, desperately trying to convince Kabir.

'You should read the history of some of India's biggest industrial houses. They all started by trading goods and then ventured into manufacturing them,' said Kabir sarcastically.

His tone further provoked Sanjeev, he replied, 'Lala *ji* would never allow this.'

'Lala *ji* is unwell and in his absence I am the boss. I have completed the formalities for setting up K.S. Traders Ltd., our new trading arm. So don't lose any sleep over this matter. It is my responsibility.'

His angry exchange with Kabir troubled Sanjeev to a great extent. Kabir's vision for the conglomerate seemed to be contrary to that conceived by the Lala and himself.

Throughout the night he was in a dilemma over whether to resign or not. Finally, he decided to wait till Khem Chand recovered from his sickness.

Khem Chand returned to the offices of Kabir and Co. after three months. The entire staff celebrated his return, cheering, distributing sweets and garlanding him. He accepted their greetings and garlands quietly. As he reached his office he gently asked his employees to leave,

'I want to speak to just Sanjeev and my son.'

After they had left, Sanjeev spoke first, 'Lala *ji* there have been some developments I want to make you aware of.'

'Daddy I can explain everything,' said Kabir confidently.

Khem Chand raised his hand, silencing both of them.

'I don't want to listen to you two fighting. You are the most valuable assets of our group and a confrontation between you will harm it's future,' he said. 'I have decided to retire completely from Kabir and Co. I will continue to be its Chairman, but both of you will actually run the show. It is time to demarcate the group's management between the two of you. Is that acceptable to both?'

'Lala *ji* whatever you decide is O.K. with me,' said Sanjeev respectfully. Kabir also nodded his head.

The Lala continued, 'Sanjeev, you will remain in your post of Managing Director of Kabir and Co. The group's iron and steel, tyres, fertilisers, sugar and chemicals companies will be under your control. These need a steady style of management and there is no one more capable than you.'

'But they constitute nearly seventy per cent of our turnover,' said Kabir, a dejected look on his face.

'My son, don't be impatient,' said Khem Chand. 'I am going to promote you. From today you are the joint Managing Director of the group. All the other companies are your exclusive responsibility.'

The next hour was spent by them going through the financial

statements of the last three months. After they had finished, Kabir excused himself, 'I have to speak to the managers I have hired.'

As Kabir closed the door behind him, Sanjeev said, 'His decision to enter into trading isn't correct and you know that.'

'I know. But I have to let him be his own man. After all, it is his first major business decision,' said Khem Chand.

'I hope your indulgence with him doesn't jeopardise the group's future or slur its reputation,' replied Sanjeev seriously.

From his substantial profits in the trading business, Kabir contributed generously to the I.L.S. campaign fund. Since most of the profits were in black money, the donation wasn't detected by either Khem Chand or Sanjeev.

The Congress party expectedly stream-rolled the opposition parties in the Lok Sabha elections. The I.L.S. was the only party, which managed to survive the onslaught, and emerged as one of the biggest non-Congress political parties in the country. The gamble in supporting the war had obviously succeeded.

Even though Rajesh Pahwa did not contest the elections, he toured extensively campaigning for his party. His oratorical skills and S.S. background had made him popular with party workers throughout India. The national media had also begun noticing and several articles on him were published in leading newspapers and magazines. Rajesh's stock within the I.L.S. had also risen dramatically after he had procured donations from Kabir. He was now considered one of the rising stars in the party.

Part Three
1974 to 1984

Seventeen

By the end of 1973, the economic situation of the country had worsened like never before. In a year, prices of food grains, petroleum and other essential commodities had almost doubled, leading to shortages and large-scale unemployment. Salaried classes were not able to make ends meet, resulting in manifold increase in industrial unrest. Profits of most major companies had plummeted worsening business confidence.

While most business houses were expecting negative growth rates, Kabir and Co. was an exception. Huge profits from K.S. Traders were offsetting the poor performance of other group companies. In just two years, the trading business had outgrown any similar operation anywhere in India.

Kabir had started off by trading in foodgrains with his father-in-law's guidance. Sahni also proved a big help as he had contacts in all major grain markets. He advised Kabir to start by creating big storage facilities. The son-in-law heeded his advice and invested heavily in building huge godowns near all major markets. Since hoarding of foodgrains was a serious offence, front men were projected as owners of the godowns. They also supervised the operation at their end and received hefty amounts for their risky services.

Most of the front men were small-time traders and S.S. sympathisers. Very soon, the business was doing so well that Kabir bought a fleet of trucks to transport the goods.

In two years Kabir had sixteen such godowns. Directly and through the front men K.S. Traders was now paying heavy bribes to corrupt officials in six states. The entire business was controlled from Kabir and Co. by a small but efficient staff of six.

Ramesh Kumar, a rustic thirty-year old fast talker, was the Chief Executive of K.S. Traders. He was a born hustler having moved from working for a small grain merchant in Hapur to his present job in a span of just four years. Sahni had recommended him for the job and even though Kabir did not trust Kumar, for K.S. Traders he was indispensable.

Kabir's stronghold over the grain markets was now so strong that other traders depended on his company to determine the prices of the black market. This peeved the centuries old traders of Nai Sarak in Old Delhi. In early 1974, several of them decided to combine and challenge the might of K.S. Traders. They knew that Kabir had secret storage facilities and they started gathering information about his godowns.

One of Kumar's former colleagues was employed by one of these traders. For a small price he spilled the beans about their gang up against K.S. Traders.

A frantic Kumar told his boss about all he had learned. 'Don't look so worried. I'll take care of them,' said Kabir confidently.

'But sir, they are very powerful people and are very close to the I.L.S. President, Narinder Singh.'

Kabir was tempted to tell his employee about his contacts, but remembering his training in Thane he kept quiet.

Rajesh Pahwa's response surprised Kabir. 'This problem cannot be solved so easily. I know about these traders. They contribute heavily to our party and are known even in Thane,' he said thoughtfully.

'If they are not stopped now, our godowns will surely be detected and then raided. I will have to respond and get their premises raided and we will all be caught in an expense raid war. All concerned will incur heavy losses,' said Kabir.

'Then, what is the solution?' asked Rajesh.

'I started this business on your advice and encouragement. Now you have to stop them,' said Kabir forcefully.

'I will have to go to Thane. Also a fresh donation from you will be required,' said Rajesh.

Kabir smiled, 'Then you should make reservations for your trip.'

This was to be Rajesh's second meeting with the old man and he was driven from the airport to the S.S. headquarters in Thane, in a car sent by the S.S. chief.

As he entered the small brightly-lit private room of the S.S.

chief, Rajesh was a bit nervous. The plain walls of the room were bright saffron and a large bed was the only furniture in it. The old man reclined on the bed in just a small loincloth. A teenage boy in the same attire was massaging his legs with oil. When Rajesh touched the patriarch's feet he could smell the almond oil the boy was using. The old man blessed Rajesh and told the boy, 'We will continue later.'

When they were alone, Patel asked Rajesh to sit down. 'I just talked to your I.L.S. President. He was adamant that we side with the traders. After all, they are old associates,' the old man said.

'Kabir made a big contribution during election time and since then, he has contributed from time to time,' reasoned Rajesh. 'He respects you a lot and when he came to know about our meeting, he gave a generous donation for the construction of our new office in Delhi.'

'What you state is correct but these traders have also contributed significantly,' said Patel.

'They represent the past while Kabir is the future. Soon, he is going to replace his father as Group Chairman of one of India's largest conglomerates. One can imagine what that means for us,' said Rajesh.

'I think you are right, I'll speak to Narindra Singh and he in turn will ask the traders to stay clear of your friend,' said the old man.

The dejected traders called on Kabir. They were greeted contemptuously by the young upstart, 'First you try to destroy my business and then you come here with your apologies.'

M C Gupta, the biggest and most respectable of the traders replied, 'We had no idea that you have the blessings of the old man in Thane. We have learnt our lesson. Please don't take this matter any further. We accept your supremacy.'

After they had left Kabir contacted Rajesh on the phone and recounted all that had happened. Rajesh laughed and said, 'Now you are the undisputed foodgrains King of India.'

'All thanks to you,' said Kabir gratefully.

Sanjeev Khanna was intelligent enough to have guessed that Kabir was hoarding illegally. He had pierced the shroud of secrecy surrounding K.S. Traders. The contractors used for constructing the godowns were associated with the group and had, over the years, dealt with Sanjeev. He was amazed at the scale on which Kabir was hoarding grains. 'If he continues like this he will be as big as the government agencies,' thought Sanjeev. But he kept his counsel. Reporting this to the government would tantamount to betraying the family to whom he owed everything. He could divulge everything to the Lala. But Khem Chand hardly ever came to the Group Head Office and was no longer interested in what transpired there.

Khem Chand had set up the Janaki Lajwanti Foundation in 1973, in memory of his departed wives. In just a few months of its inception, the Foundation was allotted land to construct a large hospital in outer Delhi.

The Lala spent most of his time at the hospital site having lost all interest in Kabir and Co. He just held a twenty per cent stake in it having transferred seventy per cent to his son. Kabir hardly ever discussed business with him. Whenever the Lala enquired about K.S. Traders, Kabir answered brusquely that it was doing well. Father and son had grown apart, with Kabir showing no interest in the Foundation and its work.

However, the Lala's relationship with his daughter-in-law had developed into a father daughter relationship. He constantly said, 'You are the daughter I always wanted.' Radhika was the one who encouraged him to go ahead with the Foundation. 'You should do something in the memories of my mother-in-laws,' she had told him.

Radhika looked after the Lala's diet, clothes and even scolded him when he spent long hours at the site. She was the only person who truly cared for him and he knew that. Her pregnancy greatly increased his fondness for her.

Kabir was happy that he would have a heir but his happiness was much less than the Lala's delight. Khem Chand started furnishing a nursery for his expected grandchild. He personally selected the furniture and the décor. One day, he entered the bungalow carrying large packets containing all sorts of toys. On another day, he bought a large number of dresses for the baby. His enthusiasm was a great source of joy for Radhika and it helped her overcome her husband's complete indifference.

Madan Mohan Sahni arrived at the Sabarwal residence a month before the due date. He had come to take Radhika to Ludhiana as it was customary for a girl to deliver her first child at her mother's house. Kabir was only too happy. For him the birth was an inconvenience he didn't want to deal with.

Khem Chand did not want his grandchild to be born away from home. But, he agreed knowing that in the absence of a woman in the house, Radhika needed her mother at the time of delivery.

Radhika gave birth to a beautiful seven-pound baby girl on 15 August 1974. The entire Sahni clan came down to Delhi for the baby's christening ceremony. Kabir was downcast on having a girl and had a perfunctory attitude towards her. Sahni had brought along with him the family priest to take out the alphabet with which the baby's name was to start, but Khem Chand put his foot down. He said, 'My daughter-in-law and I have decided on a name for her and we don't need a priest. She is a tiny light born on Independence Day. She has illuminated our house and we shall call her Deepika.'

Eighteen

In 1975, the country's economic situation continued to worsen prompting the retired socialist, Jayaprakash Narayan, to launch a movement against Mrs Gandhi. The younger cadre of the Indian Lok Sangh joined him, seeing this as the first real opportunity to unseat the Congress and capture power at the centre. The top brass of the I.L.S. considered this a violation of party discipline and took up the issue with the old man in Thane. Patel had also been contacted by J.P.'s lieutenants seeking his support. He decided to call a meeting to decide whether or not to join J.P.'s bandwagon.

More than two hundred I.L.S. leaders along with an equal number from the Swatantra Sangh attended the conclave in Thane. Lalit Shukla, the fifty-year-old I.L.S. Vice President was already an active participant in Jayaprakash's movement and spearheaded the call for joining it. He even advocated a merger with other opposition parties in order to win the next Lok Sabha elections. Rajesh Pahwa saw the benefits of joining J.P. and vigorously supported Shukla's line.

Narinder Singh, the President of the I.L.S. wanted to keep away from J.P. and he started the proceedings, speaking in his soft serious style. 'The party has always maintained an identity distinct from other political parties. We have over the years built a solid reputation. We are today known as a disciplined party with probity one, which wants to serve India's vast population rather than rule over them. With the continuing support of Patel *ji* and the S.S. we have grown to become one of India's largest political parties. I promise you, we will continue to grow. But we have to grow independently, distinctly, not as a lackey of a retired politician whose ideology is totally opposite to ours. The Swatantra Sangh has always shown us the correct path in our hour of difficulty and we hope it will do so now and ask these young people not to slur the party's name. If they continue to follow this path we will have to expel them from the party.'

As Lalit Shukla rose to speak, Pahwa led a young contingent, cheering him vociferously. Shukla was a brilliant orator who frequently resorted to theatrics to enthral his audiences. Reaching for the mike, he started by tearing up the prepared text in his hand and said dramatically, 'I had prepared this speech. But after hearing the words of our president, I think I should speak from my heart and not read from a piece of paper.'

Pahwa and his group loudly cheered his words. Raising a hand to silence them, Shukla said, 'Look at the enthusiasm of our party's young men. Should we extinguish this fire or let it spread like a forest fire, one which helps us in capturing power at the centre?' Pausing for a few seconds he continued, 'Today if we join J.P. we will surely be a part of the next central government. As for our president's words of caution about merger with other parties I can only say one thing. With Patel *ji's* and the S.S.'s guidance we will maintain our distinct identity even after we merge. We will continue to be S.S. members even after our merger and I promise that in front of all of you.'

After several other speakers had spoken about the issue, Patel got up slowly. 'We are here to serve the Hindu faith. If we are to have ministers in the Central government, it will greatly benefit our cause. I don't care what the Indian Constitution says, you must promise to be Hindus first and then Central Ministers. Shukla is right when he says that you will be able to maintain a separate identity even after a possible merger. So, I have decided that we will all support Jayaprakash Narayan.'

On returning to Delhi, Narinder Singh called a meeting of those I.L.S. leaders who were wary of supporting J.P. Seven members of the I.L.S. national committee turned up. Narinder Singh said, 'We have to take a different road from the one suggested by Patel *ji*. Shukla has become very close to J.P. He will alone wield the power and marginalise us. We are a big national party. We don't have to follow whatever Patel says.'

'We are with you,' assured the others collectively.

Within an hour of leaving the meeting, all the seven national committee members had informed Thane about Narinder Singh's act of independence.

The next day, the message of Patel was received by all major I.L.S. leaders and by evening Lalit Shukla was crowned the new party president.

*

K.S. Traders continued to flourish and Kabir continued to violate every financial law in the country. He was now simultaneously running a big money laundering operation. Large amounts of black money earned from trading business was used to purchase properties, which were later sold in white money. He was making big profits and he didn't mind paying capital gain tax. A month back Kabir had opened a Swiss bank account and was now illegally depositing some of his black money into it.

Lalit Shukla's ascent to the I.L.S. presidentship and his announcement of support to Jayaprakash, delighted Kabir. It was now almost certain that Rajesh Pahwa would become a Member of Parliament and may be even a minister in the next government.

While everything was great at work, life at home was difficult for Kabir. His relationship with Radhika had undergone a complete transformation. Before Deepkia's birth she used to constantly wait on him ready to satisfy his every need. But now she seemed to be ignoring him. Khem Chand noticed Kabir's lack of affection for his daughter. He severly reprimanded Kabir, 'It seems you don't love your daughter. You never hold her or play with her.'

'Daddy, I can't love such a small child who constantly cries and whenever you hold her you are in danger of dirtying your clothes,' said Kabir defensively.

'You were the same when you were a baby. But I loved you dearly,' said Khem Chand. 'I consider my granddaughter as the Goddess Laxmi of our house. So you dare not ignore her.'

To Kabir's surprise, he also received a mild warning from his wife. 'If you don't love Deepika, the Goddess Laxmi will get angry and you will have losses at work. Every little girl is said to be a reincarnation of her,' she said with a very serious expression on her face.

Kabir laughed at them and left for a luncheon meeting with

Rajesh Pahwa. Shukla had recently nominated Pahwa as the party secretary and they were celebrating his appointment. As they ate, Pahwa spoke without any pretentions. 'We need a large donation from you. We are launching an agitation on the first of July. We will explode railway tracks, burn buses and ransack government offices.'

'My friend, have I ever refused you? You shall have the money by 27 June,' said Kabir.

Nineteen

On 25 June, Kabir was in a late night meeting with Ramesh Kumar. The sultry June weather was making Kabir perspire even in his air-condition office.

'We are paying twelve per cent of our profits to the front men and around ten per cent goes as bribe to government officials. In 1975's six months, this expenditure has increased substantially. You should try and cut these expenses,' he said irritably.

'Believe me, sir. I have tried but the officials don't agree. They know we are earning a lot and say that we are giving them just a small part of it,' said Kumar.

Just then, there was a loud knock on the door. 'Come in,' said Kabir.

His young private secretary entered. 'Sir, I am sorry to disturb you but I have to give you the news.'

'So why don't you hurry up and tell us?' said Kabir mockingly.

'Sir, Mrs Gandhi has declared Emergency,' she said excitedly.

Kabir felt a cold sweat break out all over his body. He motioned her to leave. Looking at Kumar he said in a low voice, 'In thirty minutes I want you to prepare a list of the measures we have to take to ensure that K.S. Traders is able to function as before.'

As Kumar left, he buzzed his secretary.

'If Sanjeev Khanna is in his office, ask him to come to my office,' he said brusquely.

Kabir's message surprised Sanjeev. After all it had been quiet some time since they had even exchanged pleasantries.

As Sanjeev sat down, Kabir got straight to the point. 'You know about the imposition of Emergency?' Seeing Sanjeev nod he continued, 'I want a list of the financial curtailments that the government is likely to announce. We should take the lead in implementing everything the government orders,' he said.

'Do you think this will protect K.S. Traders,' said Sanjeev

seeing through Kabir's gameplan.

'What do you mean?' asked Kabir.

'The entire country is reeling from shortage of foodgrains and you continue to head India's biggest black marketing operation. Do you seriously expect that your godowns will never to be detected?'

'That is none of your business. Now please leave my office,' said Kabir raising his voice.

'Anything which is likely to tarnish the reputation of Kabir and Co. is my business,' he replied firmly.

'I own the business and you are just a mere employee. Don't ever forget that.'

'I implore you. Dissolve K.S. Traders or we will all be in trouble,' pleaded Sanjeev.

'You are a sissy business manager. Now, get out of my office,' shouted Kabir. Sanjeev paused for a few seconds to control the anger he felt. He realised that he was making futile attempts to make Kabir understand. The spoilt presumptuous twenty-eight-year-old would never understand that honesty and scruples were essential virtues for a successful businessman. Without a word Sanjeev Khanna got up and left the room.

'Daddy *ji*, wants to speak to you,' said Radhika as he was about to leave for work.

'I am late for a meeting in the office,' replied Kabir.

'Yesterday when he heard about the Emergency, he spoke to several ministers and he wants to tell you about it.'

Kabir became interested in what his father wanted to tell him, 'Where is he?' he asked.

Khem Chand was sitting in his study reading a newspaper from among the stack on his desk. Seeing Kabir, he asked his son to sit down. He started by pointing out an article in a leading daily supporting Mrs Gandhi's step. Kabir read a few lines and then said, 'It seems you support the Emergency.'

The Lala replied slowly, carefully choosing his words, 'Son, I don't have to support or oppose the Emergency. I am a businessman and not a politician. Do not ever forget that you too are the same.'

Kabir did not respond and Khem Chand continued, 'Last

night, I spoke to some of my minister friends. I feared nationalism of some industries but they have given their word that no such steps are planned. They have also assured me that honest industrialists will not be bothered, only unscrupulous business enterprises will be raided. Now tell me honestly, is there anything illegal in K.S. Traders' operations.'

Kabir knew that his father would not believe a simple denial. He called for Radhika to bring his daughter. She promptly returned holding the girl to her chest.

Dramatically Kabir took Deepika from her. Holding her affectionately he placed his hand on her head, 'I swear on the life of my daughter. There is nothing illegal about K.S. Traders.'

Even a week after the Emergency had been declared, Kabir had not been able to get in touch with Rajesh. Repeated calls to Rajesh's party office and home had proved futile. Even the ailing senior Pahwa was not available. Kabir was convinced they had gone underground fearing arrest.

On 3 July, he received a phone call late in the night. 'Your dearest friend wants to meet you. Be in front of your college tomorrow night at nine p.m. sharp.'

All alone, Kabir was in front of St. Stephens at the designated time. The road was deserted and he was reminded of the night he had killed Shakeel and Mary. A few minutes had passed when in the rear view mirror he saw a car stop. Pahwa got out of the car and quickly got into his car. 'Drive away.' was all he said.

Pahwa kept looking back for the next several minutes. Satisfied that no one was following them, he seemed to relax and asked, 'How have you been?'

Kabir laughed at his friend's query and said, 'For more than a week, I have been trying to speak to you. Where have you been and where is Pahwa Uncle?'

'My father is in Thane and I have been at a supporter's house in Ghaziabad. But he is a known S.S. man so it is no longer safe there. I have been made in charge of agitations in western Uttar Pradesh. So, I need a hideaway not too far from Delhi.'

'Opposition governments are in power in Gujarat and Tamil Nadu. So why are you hiding?' asked Kabir.

'The government considers our party to be a threat to the so-called secular fabric of the country. We are actively agitating and very soon we are all going to be arrested,' Rajesh explained.

'Well, if you wish to hide I have just the right locale for you.'

'Where?' asked Rajesh once again looking over his shoulder.

His friend's paranoia amused Kabir. 'Our farm in Kotdwara is the ideal hideaway. It is not too far from Delhi and no one goes there except the local villagers. Tomorrow morning I will make the arrangements,' he said.

*

A couple of months into the Emergency, K.S. Traders' front men were understandably nervous. They wanted to empty the godowns and stop further hoarding. Ramesh Kumar communicated their views to his boss. Kabir became livid with anger, 'How dare they demand the end of the entire business? They have earned lacs and at the slightest hint of trouble they want to desert us.'

'Calm down, they have not deserted us. They are afraid and just need reassurance from us,' said Kumar.

'They seem to be working in tandem,' said Kabir.

'No way. Some of them don't even know the existence of the others. However, there is a similarity in their reasons for requesting closure.'

'What is that?' asked Kabir.

'State Government officials have stopped accepting bribes. They are frightened because of the Emergency.'

Kabir asked worriedly, 'The godowns are spread across six different states. How is it possible that these officials have suddenly become honest?'

Kumar explained, 'A corrupt government servant will accept bribes only till his job isn't in danger. Since the Emergency, a slight complaint can seriously affect their career.'

'What about the ones in Delhi?'

'They have started saying that it would be better if we curtailed our business for a while. However, they are still demanding heavy bribes,' said Kumar.

'Tell the front men, come what may I will not shut down their operations. If they are so afraid then they should return ownership of the godowns. We will find people to replace them,' said Kabir ending the conversation.

On 30 November 1975, M C Gupta, the biggest among the grain merchants of old Delhi, was raided by officials of the Ministry of Food and Civil Supplies. Years of political patronage by local I.L.S. leaders had made him careless and from his premises, a number of incriminating documents and black market records were seized by the raiding party. Gupta was arrested and his interrogation began.

The raid party was led by a joint director in the Ministry, Majid Mohammad Siddiqui, a young Indian Administrative Services officer. The son of a former bureaucrat, his integrity and strictness had made him a feared officer wherever he had been posted. Posted in his present job days after the imposition of Emergency, Siddiqui had the green signal to go after any black marketer, however powerful he may be. Siddiqui personally supervised Gupta's interrogation.

'I have a lot of patience. I won't stop till you give the names of all the top black marketers and corrupt government officials,' he told Gupta after two days of interrogation.

Gupta was sixty years old and was finding it difficult to continue in his present state. His cell was small and filthy. He had trouble sleeping on the hard bed and eating the jail food. He knew that his only way out was giving some information to his interrogators.

'I can't tell about my friends and associates but I can help you net the king of all black marketers and hoarders,' he told Siddiqui. 'But after I tell you I have to be released on bail.'

'Mr Gupta, you are not in a position to bargain. But if this person is a big fish then we may agree to your request,' said Siddiqui.

'His operations extend all over North India. His name is Kabir Sabarwal, son of Lala Khem Chand, heir to India's eighth biggest industrial empire,' said Gupta, pleased that his information had taken Siddiqui completely by surprise. Hiding his excitement Siddiqui asked Gupta to detail Kabir's operations.

Gupta told Siddiqui everything he knew, 'His company is

called K.S. Traders Ltd. It started operations just after the war with Pakistan. At first we didn't take him seriously, that was our first mistake. The boy spent big money in constructing godowns from Bihar to Rajasthan. I have information about some of them but, on the records, he doesn't own them. His business has become so successful that he sets the black market prices. Last year, we tried to take him on but he managed to put pressure on us and we had to buckle under that pressure.'

'Who did he use to pressurise you?' asked Siddiqui.

Gupta lowered his head and spoke in a low voice, 'The S.S. chief, K B Patel.'

'It is hard to believe what Gupta has told you,' said Siddiqui's boss. 'How can the son of a prominent industrialist be close to the fascist S.S.?'

'Whether Gupta is telling the truth or not, we have to initiate an investigation on Kabir Sabarwal and his company,' said Siddiqui.

'You are right. Co-ordinate with Sunil Kathuria, the intelligence officer who has recently joined our department. For an investigation of this size, we need him.'

After just a week of investigation into K.S. Traders, Sunil Kathuria was surprised by what his seven member team was unearthing. He put in a request for at least twenty additional personnel.

*

Khem Chand's Janaki Lajwanti Charitable Hospital in Trans Yamuna was nearing completion. He had pulled out all stops in its construction. It's beautiful white building with sprawling lawns, spacious wards and state-of-the-art medical equipment were a great source of pride for him. Khem Chand had roped in one of Delhi's most respected doctors to be its chief. Several other prominent doctors had followed and now the hospital had one of the capital's best panel of doctors and surgeons.

The Lala told Radhika about his plans for its inauguration. 'It will be a grand affair. The President will cut the ribbon and then at least a thousand people will be served lunch. I have also talked to several social workers. We will admit only the poorest of the poor.'

Radhika smiled, pleased at her father-in-law's benevolence and asked, 'Have you decided on a date?'

'I estimate everything to be ready by the first of March,' he replied, 'One thing bothers me. Who will look after the hospital after I die?'

Radhika pondered over his question for a few seconds and replied, 'Deepika will. I want her to become a doctor when she grows up.'

Twenty

By the end of January 1976, Siddiqui and Kathuria had completed their investigations on Kabir and K.S. Traders. Key executives and fourteen of his godowns had been identified. They had ample evidence that the front men were fronts and Kabir owned the godowns. Phone taps on the offices of K.S. Traders and houses of Kabir and Ramesh Kumar had provided enough evidence to prosecute everyone involved in the black marketing. Kathuria had also uncovered Kabir's elaborate money laundering scheme and informed Income Tax officials. They were eagerly awaiting the green signal to pounce on Kabir. Kathuria had, on the orders of Siddiqui, conducted a thorough investigation of other group companies but everything about them was above board.

A final meeting was held to decide the day Kabir and his company were to be raided. Top officials of every financial enforcement agency attended. It was to be massive co-ordinated effort in six different states and all details were gone through.

Ramesh Kumar had been born in a tiny hut in his village near the Hapur market. At the age of eighteen he had completed whatever little education was available in his village. He joined his illiterate father in the family line of loading and unloading sacks of wheat. In his spare time he used his limited education to learn the grain trade. In a few years, a trader impressed by his knowledge of the quality of grains, gave him a small clerical job. In a couple of years, Kumar was running the entire business. It was then that he came in contact with Madan Mohan Sahni. Sahni regularly visited the Hapur market and noticed the bright young man. Kumar knew about Sahni's wealth and did his utmost to impress the businessman. Sahni saw the burning ambition in the boy's heart and told him, 'One day I will find a job befitting your intelligence and knowledge.' A year later he heard from Sahni. 'My son-in-law is opening a trading company. I want you to head its operations,' he offered.

In just four years, K.S. Traders had changed his whole life. He had prospered incredibly. His rustic wife now spoke English and dressed finely. His son and daughter now went to Delhi's best public school. Kumar had earned enough to purchase a decent plot in upmarket Greater Kailash. Proud of the acquisition, he spent lavishly on constructing and decorating a beautiful house. Completing the house was a great source of joy for him. Every day, as he left for office, Kumar would turn back to look at it fondly.

On 12 February, he repeated his daily habit as he got into his car. As he started to put it into first gear several men entered his driveway through the open gate. One of them in a dark leather jacket approached him. Kumar lowered his glass window. 'Mr Ramesh Kumar,' the man enquired.

'Yes, what can I do for you?' asked Kumar.

'We are from the Ministry of Food and Civil, this is a raid,' the man answered gravely.

Khem Chand was having breakfast when the Chowkidar ushered the men in. He was surprised to see fifteen to twenty men enter his drawing room. Slowly, getting up he asked them, 'Whom do you want to meet?'

'Mr Sabarwal, we want to meet your son Kabir Sabarwal,' said one of the men.

'But who are you?' asked Khem Chand.

'We are with the Ministry of Food and Civil, this is a raid. Now can we please meet your son.'

Khem Chand had never been raided by any government agency. But he kept calm, confident that his son was doing nothing wrong.

'Kabir left a hour ago,' he answered.

On hearing Khem Chand's answer the government men panicked visibly. 'Where did he go?' several of them asked in unison.

'He didn't say, but he will soon reach his office. Would you like some breakfast before you start your work?'

Kabir had left home early because Vipin Sharma, one of Rajesh Pahwa's confidants, had summoned him. They met at

Buddha Jayanti Park.

'Rajesh *ji's* father has sent me. Many of our men are in hiding and their families are finding it difficult to make ends meet. They need money.' Kabir had to check whether Vipin had been truly sent by his friend's father. 'Where did you meet Pahwa *ji*?' he asked.

'I didn't meet him. He called from Thane,' replied Vipin.

Vipin had checked out and Kabir promised him some money by evening.

On Barakhamba Road, Kabir encountered a traffic jam. Spotting a traffic policeman, he asked him, 'There is never such a jam on this road. What is the matter?' The policeman answered, 'The government is raiding one of the buildings. They have surrounded it. None of the employees or their vehicles are being allowed inside.'

'Which building is being raided?' Kabir asked casually.

'Kabir House,' was the reply.

Kabir began to sweat even in the cold morning. He realised that if he stayed in the car he had no chance of escape. The traffic was so slow that he would surely be recognised when he drove past his building. He checked his wallet, it contained about three thousand rupees, enough to help him escape. He opened the car door, getting out he slowly crossed to the other side of the road. He started walking in the direction opposite to his office building, desperately controlling the urge to walk faster. After walking for about five minutes, he pondered over what kind of transport to use. If he hired a taxi, the driver would remember where he was dropped. Since no one would ever imagine him taking a bus, he decided to take the next Delhi Transport Corporation bus.

In an hour he had changed buses and was travelling in a Uttar Pradesh Roadways bus en route to Kotdwara.

The raids were a feather in the cap of every senior officer who participated in them. More than enough evidence was gathered to incriminate all involved in the black marketing racket. Only the search of the Sabarwal residence hadn't yielded any evidence. Thirteen of the front men and Ramesh Kumar, along with his entire staff were behind bars. Thousands of tons of grains were seized and the government agencies were still on the look out for more of Kabir's godowns.

The only disappointment had been the lucky escape of the prime accused, Kabir Sabarwal. His abandoned car had been found just two hundred metres from his office building. Even a week after the raids they had no idea where he was.

The news of the illegality of K.S. Traders devastated Khem Chand and shook the business world. The impeccable reputation of Kabir and Co. built in three decades was discredited in a day. Khem Chand had to shelve his hospital's inauguration plan. What troubled him the most was that Kabir had falsely sworn on the life of his only child. Radhika was badly shaken up by her husband's misdeeds. She knew that if anything were to happen to the Lala, the entire conglomerate would fall apart. She also realised that in this critical time he needed her full support.

'Your son has failed you, but I will not. He has shamed you but I promise, my daughter will do you proud,' she said giving him hope to fight on. The Lala needed no encouragement, he loved his granddaughter more than anything else.

'I know she will,' he said affectionately.

Khem Chand knew that he had to rise from his self-imposed retirement and control the damage caused by his son. He once again took control of Kabir and Co. He fully co-operated with the investigating agencies realising that any cover up would be futile as a lot had already been discovered.

Siddiqui and Kathuria were wary of Khem Chand's genuine attempts to assist in their continuing investigation.

'Your son has been missing for a week. Hasn't he made any contact?' asked Kathuria.

'No, I don't think he will contact me,' replied Khem Chand.

'But your daughter-in-law must be worried sick about him. When he contacts either of you, do inform us immediately.'

The Lala looked straight into Kathuria's eyes and said, 'Son, in 1947 I came to Delhi penniless. Today I am the Chairman of Kabir and Co. It has seventeen subsidiaries and not one of them was ever raided in the past. Not one case of Income Tax or any such matter is pending against them. My son must be punished and if he contacts me or my daughter-in-law, your people will be the first to know.'

Khem Chand's firm words sobered up the two officers. Siddiqui said, 'We are very sorry but you have to understand the circumstances. Kabir ran the country's biggest black marketing racket.

Khem Chand accepted their apology and the questioning continued.

*

Kabir had arrived at his Kotdwara farm late in the evening. Rajesh had been surprised by his friend's unexpected arrival and had greeted him with joy.

'I was getting totally bored. But why did you come by bus?' he asked Kabir.

Kabir slumped into an armchair and started to recount the day's events. Towards the end of his account he mentioned the monetary losses. 'I had earned between five to six crores through this business. Now it will be siezed by the government. So much hard work has gone waste,' despaired Kabir.

'I know it is a big loss but you have to get over it,' sympathised Rajesh.

'I haven't told you the worst part,' said Kabir. 'A strict joint director had recently been posted. You want to know his name?'

'What difference will his name make?' asked Rajesh.

'His name is M M Siddiqui.'

Pahwa's face contorted with anger, 'Now I understand everything. The raids were a conspiracy between the Muslims and the Congress government. I promise you when we come to power, I will destroy that Muslim officer and all who have dared to raid you.'

'But what do we do today? I am a fugitive from the law,' said Kabir.

'Welcome to the club, you are not alone. There is a warrant out for me from the past two weeks. How much money have you got?'

'I have just three thousand rupees. We have a bank account in Kotdwara town. It must have at least five thousand,' replied Kabir.

Rajesh shook his head. 'It is too risky, you can't operate the bank account. Don't worry, three thousand is enough to get us where I plan to take you.'

'If we could leave the country, money will not be a problem. I have about forty lacs stashed in a Swiss Bank account,' said Kabir.

Rajesh clapped his hands in joy and patted Kabir's back, 'You are cunning and intelligent, a true S.S. man. I have one last agitation planned in five days. After that, both of us will cross the border into Nepal. Can you access your account from there?'

'I will need to open a bank account. Do you have any contacts in Kathmandu?' asked Kabir.

'The Nepalese chief of the S.S. is Man Chand Bahadur, a multimillionaire and he will be our host.'

Rajesh's last agitation before his departure was a big success. I.L.S. and other opposition parties organised a violent demonstration in Moradabad town diverting the police's attention, while Rajesh and a small band of arsonists blew up railway tracks at several places.

That evening, the two fugitives boarded a Roadways bus. Changing three buses by the next evening, they were in Bahraich just a few kilometres from the border and by nightfall they reached Nepalganj, the first Nepalese town across the border. As they descended the bus steps, a smartly dressed Nepalese man approached.

'I have been sent by Shri Man Chand to take you to Kathmandu. Come, my car is parked just outside the bus terminal.'

Man Chand Bahadur turned out to be a warm, rotund sixty-year-old. His bearing was contrary to all S.S. men Kabir had ever encountered. He dressed garishly and wore heavy gold chains around his neck. He had seven adult children from three wives and the whole family welcomed them with open arms. Bahadur had reserved a wing of his opulent house for his guest and designated two servants for their care. 'This part of the house has a separate entrance just in case you bring personal guests,' Bahadur said with a wink.

In a week, the two fugitives settled down enjoying Bahadur's hospitality. Kabir was still disappointed on losing crores. Pahwa sensed his friend's feelings and said, 'Forget about what you have lost. Imagine how much you will gain when the I.L.S. comes to power.'

Following Rajesh's telephonic instructions, Vipin Sharma called on the Lala ten days after Kabir's escape.

'Your son is safe and well,' he said.

'Where is he? When can I meet him?' asked Khem Chand.

'I am afraid I have no idea about his whereabouts,' said Sharma.

'The next time he contacts you, tell my son it is in his interest if he surrenders. Being a fugitive will adversely affect his case.'

'I will communicate your instructions,' said Sharma.

Twenty One

It took months for Khem Chand and Sanjeev to gain back the confidence of their employees, dealers and business associates. However, they were not too successful in mending their previously smooth relationship with the government departments because of Kabir's escape from the law. Every tax return filed by the group was viewed with suspicion and thoroughly investigated. Khem Chand spent long hours at the office and his only joy at the end of the day was the sight of Deepika. The child had become increasingly attached to her grandfather and craved for his attention. On several instances, he had to cancel important evening meetings on receiving Radhika's phone call. 'She isn't sleeping, she keeps on crying and saying Dada Dada.'

It had been more than six months since husband and wife had seen each other. The Lala knew that Radhika was too old fashioned to stop loving Kabir and awaited his return. He was worried that his son's nonchalance was beginning to affect her mental state.

The day after Deepika's second birthday, Radhika asked her father-in-law, 'If he returns, will he be arrested immediately?' Khem Chand nodded his head.

'Why don't you forgive him and get the charges dropped?'

'I can't help him. They have too much evidence against him,' said Khem Chand.

'When I was a little girl, I looked up to my father. I thought the world of him despite his many flaws. I want Deepika to have a normal life, she shouldn't grow up thinking that her father is a criminal,' said Radhika, tears beginning to pour from her eyes.

Khem Chand replied carefully, 'I want Deepika to have a normal life, as much you. But I can't interfere in Kabir's matter.'

'Daddy *ji*, you are the most intelligent, experienced and influential person I know. If you had exerted yourself, Kabir would have been home for his daughter's birthday,' she said, leaving his room.

Khem Chand's principles did not allow him to manipulate people on Kabir's behalf. For a week, he pondered over Radhika's words and decided that he could not let his daughter-in-law live her life without her husband.

Sahni had suffered big losses when his black marketing racket had been shut down because of the Emergency. He was in Delhi for a relative's wedding and was surprised when the Lala invited him for lunch at a Connaught Place restaurant. As soon as they were seated, Khem Chand got straight to the point.

'Sahni *ji*, I know you helped Kabir in setting up K.S. Traders. Now you have to help in ensuring his return.'

'Lala *ji,* I am sorry about what has happened but no one could foresee the Emergency. I...'

Khem Chand interrupted him, 'I am not blaming you for what you did. Kabir is a grown man and should be held accountable for his actions. I am only interested in meeting Ramesh Kumar.'

'I thought he was in jail,' said Sahni.

'He was released on bail about a month back and seems to have returned to his native village.'

'Lala *ji*, I'll find him for you,' promised Sahni.

Sahni reached the Hapur grain market early in the morning and went straight to Anil Goel, Kumar's previous employer.

'Kumar drinks all day and rarely ventures out of his village,' said Goel.

'I want to meet him in whatever state he is,' said Sahni. 'Can you take me to his village?'

'Yes, it is just eight kilometres from here.'

Passing through the village's bylanes, they arrived at Kumar's tiny house. Goel knocked on the door, an elderly woman came out. 'We want to meet Ramesh,' said Goel.

They were led into a small room, the woman pointed to a figure lying on a cot. 'Wake him up, if you can,' she said.

Goel shook Kumar and asked him to wake up. Slowly Kumar rose from his slumber. Sahni was aghast at his appearance. Kumar's unshaved face looked haggard, his clothes were torn in several places and he smelt of country made liquor. Recognising them he asked in a hoarse voice, 'What brings you here?'

'Get ready I have to take you with me,' said Sahni.

Sahni called the Lala from Goel's shop. 'I have him with me. In about four hours we will be at the Rajdhani Guest House in Trans Yamuna. Have you seen it?'

'I will be there,' said Khem Chand.

The Lala was waiting in the Guest House lobby to receive them.

Ramesh touched his feet, 'Lala *ji,* I am honoured that you sent for me.'

Khem Chand patted the young man's shoulder, 'Come, we'll talk in the room I have booked for you.' After they had settled, Khem Chand asked Ramesh, 'You don't look too well. Tell me all that has happened in the past seven months.'

Ramesh failed to control his emotions as he recounted the events since the raids. After being arrested from his residence, he had been taken for interrogation to the Ministry. After a full day of questioning he was taken in front of a judge who rejected his bail application and sent him to Tihar Central Jail. In the meantime, all his illegally gained assets were seized. His wife and children had to move into a friend's apartment in Ghaziabad. They were still there surviving on his friend's mercy. He was granted bail after spending six months in the jail. Penniless and unable to face his wife, he had quietly returned to his village.

'You have spent seven unfortunate months. But your luck is about to change. Lala *ji* has found a way out for you,' said Sahni.

Turning to the Lala, Kumar desperately said, 'My children haven't gone to school for the past seven months, my wife is living on just one saree. I will do anything you ask me to do.'

'Kabir is absconding ever since the raids and will not return till his name is cleared. You have to confess in front of the authorities that the entire black marketing racket was yours. You were dealing on behalf of the front men and Kabir had no knowledge about your activities. As it is, you are bound to be sentenced to seven years and after this confession you will still get the same,' said the Lala.

'What do I get for my efforts?' asked Ramesh.

'If you do as I have told you, I will pay you enough to buy a house and start afresh.' Kumar was surprised by Khem Chand's generous offer and said, 'Kabir *ji* used to say that you never compromised on your principles. Perhaps your love for your son is making you do all this.'

'What Kabir said is correct, but I can't let my daughter-in-law and granddaughter suffer because of him.'

Ramesh Kumar's confession took Siddiqui completely by surprise. The officer thundered at Khem Chand, 'I will still prove that your son ran the entire racket. I am sure you have taken advantage of Kumar's poor financial position.'

Khem Chand replied evasively, 'I have done no such thing. My son's application for anticipatory bail is coming up. I implore you not to oppose it.'

'Lala *ji*, I cannot be bought like Ramesh Kumar. I will use all my official strength to press for "no bail" for your son.'

Siddiqui was true to his words. Khem Chand's battery of lawyers were unable to get anticipatory bail.

*

In Kathmandu, Kabir and Rajesh followed the events through Indian newspapers and regular reports from Vipin Sharma. The Lala's decision to pay off Ramesh Kumar had surprised Kabir. A hope had been kindled in him but the rejection of his bail plea, once again disheartened him.

'Your father's intentions are right but his strategy is all wrong,' commented Rajesh.

'What strategy should he adopt?' asked Kabir.

'After Kumar's confession, the only problem is Siddiqui. Lala *ji* should go on the offensive and seek to discredit the Muslim. If reports are published that he is an extortionist and targeted you just for money, he will be discredited and transferred from his present post.'

'My father has never been a manipulator. All you say is beyond him.'

'I know about Lala *ji* but what about your father-in-law. He can easily accomplish the task,' said Rajesh.

'What if Siddiqui isn't transferred even after that?' asked Kabir.

'Then there is another method, I'll tell Sahni *ji* about it.'

Sahni followed the instructions from Kathmandu and within a fortnight several newspaper reports were published against Siddiqui. But his reputation was unaffected and he wasn't transferred. It was then that Sahni delivered the fatal blow.

Two lac rupees in cash was deposited in the joint savings account of Mrs and Mr Majid Mohammad Siddiqui and the authorities were informed about it. The Central Bureau of Investigation moved quickly and raids were conducted on Siddiqui. His accounts were sealed and he was arrested for having unaccountable money.

Siddiqui's incarceration was a boon for Kabir. He was potrayed as a victim of overzealous, corrupt officers hounding a prominent industrialist to further their careers and extort bribes. On New Year's Eve, all charges against him were dropped.

As Kabir made preparations to leave for Delhi, Rajesh issued last minute instructions, 'Remember what I told you. Act like a son ashamed of his previous acts. Be dutiful towards your family and do not disagree with your father even on trivial issues.'

Twenty Two

In February 1977, Mrs Gandhi unexpectedly lifted the Emergency and announced Lok Sabha elections, taking the opposition completely by surprise. All the opposition leaders, including Lalit Shukla, knew they had to move quickly and merged to form the Janta Party. Rajesh Pahwa received a hero's welcome on his return from Kathmandu and was promptly made the party's candidate from one of Delhi's seven Parliamentary constituencies.

The Janata Party swept the polls and in the northern states it won almost all the seats. For the first time since Independence, a non-Congress government came to power in the Centre. Rajesh Pahwa won from his constituency by an all time high margin. The new Prime Minister, Morarji Desai included Lalit Shukla and six other former I.L.S. leaders in his Council of Ministers.

For Kabir, the poll results were like a long awaited dream coming true. He had spent almost his entire savings in the Swiss account to bankroll the party's campaign in Delhi and it was time to reap the fruits of power. Khem Chand was unshaken by the results. 'This motley combination of ideologically opposed parties will never be able to administrate effectively. This government will sink weighed by its internal contradictions,' he commented.

'But Daddy, we should be proud that democracy is alive and well in India. The Emergency had throttled freedom. Now the first non-Congress government is in power,' said Kabir.

Khem Chand laughed loudly. 'If Mrs Gandhi had throttled freedom then the Janata Party would never have been allowed to win. As for this being a non-Congress government, I can only laugh at your political naivety. The Prime Minister and most of his cabinet colleagues are former Congress leaders.'

Kabir kept quiet continuing his month long charade of being the dutiful son. Since his return from Kathmandu, he spent almost all his spare time with the family. Even in the election campaign he had purposely feigned indifference towards Rajesh

Pahwa knowing that it would impress his father. Kabir's open show of affection for Deepika and Radhika pleased the Lala and in May, he was reappointed Kabir and Co.'s Joint Managing Director.

Rajesh congratulated him, 'You are back in the saddle after the tumultuous events of the past fifteen months. Tomorrow I have arranged a special meeting for you. Be at my North Avenue apartment at six in the evening.' The meeting turned out be a gathering of several key ministers and important Members of Parliament. Pahwa introduced Kabir, 'He is my best friend and heir to the Sabarwal empire. He is an old financier and supporter of our party. Any request from his is to be granted immediately.'

Kabir and Co. had been stagnating for the past three financial years and Kabir's political connections gave it the boost it needed. Entering the unchartered arena of government contracting, Kabir convinced his father to go in for large contracts of all that the conglomerate produced. In order to expand existing production facilities and venture into new industries, licences were required from the Central Government. Rajesh's machinations ensured that his friend would be the first to get the licences and outstrip his rivals.

Kabir and Co. retained its lost glory when the results for the year 1978-79 were announced. Four years after it had slipped out of the list of the country's top business houses, it once again retained its previous rank of being the eighth biggest. Kabir's diligence and ability to manipulate the government impressed his staunchest critic. Khanna told Khem Chand, 'Lala *ji*, I have to grudgingly admit I was wrong about Kabir. Today he is the most brilliant young industrialist in the country.'

Khem Chand agreed with his top employee, 'It seems initially he wrongly channelised his energy and now it is flowing in the right direction.'

Kabir was enjoying the adulation and admiration showered on him from all quarters. One newspaper report called him 'the come-back kid' and another called him 'the brilliant son sure to outshine his illustrious father.'

Kabir's only disappointment was that their second born was also a girl. Hiding his true feelings, he welcomed the child's birth and gave a huge party on her christening day. Khem Chand selected a suitable name for his second granddaughter. 'Her birth is lucky for her father. We shall call her Bhagyashree.'

In June 1979, Khem Chand was striken by malaria and had to be hospitalised. The disease weakened him considerably. On his return home, he spoke to Kabir, 'I am sixty-seven years old. It is time for me to completely retire from the company and expend all my energy in charitable work.'

'But I will feel helpless without you,' said Kabir hiding his happiness.

'My mind is made up. I am going to transfer all my balance holdings to Deepika and Bhagyashree, in your guardianship.'

A week later Khem Chand left for Calcutta to scout for a suitable location for his new hospital project.

Kabir now controlled ninety per cent of Kabir and Co. and started reorganising its board. Kabir's ultimate aim was getting rid of Sanjeev Khanna, and for that to be possible he needed to replace the directors. Kabir called each director separately and asked him to resign. The next day Sanjeev Khanna barged into his office.

'You have no right to humiliate the directors. I know you are doing this just to remove me,' he said angrily.

'When you know what I want, why don't you resign?'

'I will resign only after I speak to Lala *ji*. I want his contact number in Calcutta,' demanded Sanjeev.

'He isn't a shareholder any ore and therefore there is no need for you to speak to him,' said Kabir. 'You have twenty-four hours to resign or you will be unceremoniously chucked out of Kabir and Co.'

Sanjeev Khanna had spent thirty years of his life in nurturing the conglomerate, but it took his secretary just three minutes to type his resignation. With a heavy heart, he cleared his desk and packed his personal belongings. Several important executives called on him and said, 'We will all leave with you. Without your guidance we can no longer continue here.' Their loyalty made Sanjeev emotional. 'I am tired of being in the same post for the past thirty years. I need a new challenge, but all of you have a long career ahead,' he said.

Kabir no longer had to continue acting like a dutiful husband and caring father. Radhika was surprised at his changed behaviour and asked him. 'What is wrong? All of a sudden you have stopped spending time with your daughters. You hardly speak to me. Have I done something wrong?' Kabir didn't say a word and left the room.

The exit of Sanjeev Kumar was a high point in Kabir's life. Finally, he had total control over the conglomerate and was free to use its immense power. However, political events dampened his triumph.

Towards the end of July, Khem Chand's prediction about the Janata Party became true. Prime Minister Morarji Desai resigned and was replaced by Choudhury Charan Singh. The Indian Lok Sangh component of the Janata Party was out of power and unclear about its future strategy. Rajesh told Kabir, 'Our image has been tarnished because of our association with other parties. We are bound to perform badly in the next elections.'

'The election is two years away. Surely by then you will be able to regain your independent status,' said Kabir.

'Mark my words, the Congress wants an election by December.'

The Lok Sabha elections of December 1979 were a massive mandate in Mrs Gandhi's favour. The Indian electorate reposed its faith in her leadership, vanquishing most opposition stalwarts. The I.L.S. performed as expected. It now had just fifteen representatives in the Lok Sabha. Rajesh Pahwa's defeat was a major blow to Kabir. But Pahwa was unfazed by it. 'Don't worry, we'll bounce back,' he told Kabir.

Khem Chand was pleased by the election results. He lectured Kabir on the advantages of a Congress government. 'After two and a half years of non-governance, we will at last enjoy stability. Never forget that political stability is necessary for any business to prosper. I have heard that the government is accepting applications for foreign joint venture proposals. We should not lag behind.'

Kabir was peeved by his father's praise of the Congress. 'It took us more than two hundred years to get rid of the British and now you want us to be enslaved once again,' he said angrily.

'Don't talk like a Swantantra Sangh fanatic. How can foreign tie-ups enslave the country?'

'The East India Company was also a foreign company and it ended up ruling the country,' said Kabir forcefully.

'That was years ago. To progress, we need foreign companies, especially in high technology industries,' said the Lala.

'Any future decision for Kabir and Co. is my prerogative. You need not worry about it.'

Twenty Three

Between 1980 and 1984, the Indian economy witnessed all round growth. Industrial and agricultural production increased at a healthy rate and numerous industrial projects were on the anvil. Inflation was in check, savings increased and a stock market culture started developing. The 1983 Asian Games in Delhi boosted India's image at home and abroad. Kabir and Co. grew with the economy and maintained its position.

The Indian Lok Sangh continued to be gripped by organisational and ideological problems. A Congress victory in February 1983 in Delhi's Municipal and Metropolitan elections had seen its last bastion crumble. The new S.S. chief, Ram Das Deshmukh, considered Lalit Shukla to be a poor organiser and just a good speaker. 'He should have joined films. I am sure his theatrical skills would be of use there,' commented Deshmukh.

When the Indian Army entered the Golden Temple in Operation Bluestar, Shukla supported the action. Some I.L.S. leaders were surprised by his response and took up the issue with Deshmukh. They were in for a shock. The patriarch shared Shukla's viewpoint. Deshmukh's logic was simple. 'If it becomes an issue of Hindus versus Sikhs, we have to help the government in protecting the Hindus. Also, as a nationalist organisation we have to oppose terrorism,' said the S.S. chief.

'I think you should send a senior S.S. leader to Punjab to assess the situation on the spot and receive feedback from our cadres,' requested Kishen Kumar, a general secretary of the I.L.S. Kishen was a protégé of Deshmukh and the patriarch agreed to his request. He delegated S N Pahwa to visit Punjab as his observer.

Pahwa stayed at Sahni's residence in Ludhiana on the last leg of his extensive tour. Sahni took him in his car to visit the S.S. office. As the driver parked the car, a couple of men approached it from both sides. Reaching the car, one of them waited while the other tapped on Pahwa's window. 'Are you Surindra Nath Pahwa?' he asked. Pahwa replied in the affirmative. The man reached into his shirt and taking out a revolver fired at him. The first bullet hit Pahwa on the face while the second one entered his brain. Sahni was in shock and unable to move. The assassin slowly turned the revolver's barrel at him and fired.

The double assassination devastated Kabir. Both the dead persons had been there for him, whenever help was required. The Lala grieved for his daughter-in-law's loss but was surprised at the connection between the father of Rajesh Pahwa and Sahni. Radhika had fainted when she heard the news and was advised a week's bed rest by the doctor. Sahni was cremated in Ludhiana but S N Pahwa's body was brought to Delhi. His body was taken to the Nigambodh Ghat in a huge procession. Every known S.S. and I.L.S. leader of Delhi participated.

The Swatantra Sangh decided to organise a rally in Delhi fifteen days after Sahni's death. It was a big success. Thousands attended from Delhi, Punjab, Haryana and Uttar Pradesh. Rajesh Pahwa was cheered by the crowds as he was the first speaker. 'I know my father's blood will not go waste,' he said emotionally. 'On behalf of the I.L.S., I demand that the Central Government issue gun licences to our cadres in Punjab.'

Lalit Shukla's dramatic oratory failed to enthral the workers and he was jeered by the large crowd.

Kishen Kumar gave a rousing speech, 'Those of us who suffered the horrors of Partition do not want our children to grow up in a similar situation. I request Mrs Gandhi to arm our cadres.'

Mrs Gandhi's assassination shocked the nation. The people of Delhi reacted with different emotions. Some refused to believe the news. Some sobbed, giving full vent to their grief, while others reacted furiously unleashing the animal, which lies dormant in every human being. As riots ravaged the city, Khem Chand pleaded with Kabir and Radhika to let him out of the house. 'I must do something to help, thousands are dying. Let me go out.'

Kabir said, 'What can you do? It is the police's job.'

'I know what riots are. When that fever grips a man's brain, he loses his sanity and goes berserk. I am an old man. People will surely listen to what I say,' said the Lala.

'Daddy *ji*, your life is too precious for us. We can't let you risk it,' said Radhika.

All pollsters predicted a win for the Congress led by the new Prime Minister Rajiv Gandhi. The sympathy generated by Mrs Gandhi's assassination and the Prime Minister's youthful clean image delivered a fatal double blow to opposition stalwarts. The mandate received by the Congress was the best ever performance by any party. The I.L.S. was routed in the Lok Sabha elections. Its president, Lalit Shukla, lost by a big margin. It was the party's worst performance since its inception.

As Rajiv Gandhi's first cabinet was sworn in, euphoria gripped the nation. A new phase of industrial liberalisation was expected to begin and boost the economy. To take advantage of the situation, Kabir decided to further diversify the conglomerate and expand most of its existing production facilities.

Part Four
1985 to 1990

Twenty Four

The Indian Lok Sangh's electoral rout provided the ammunition Deshmukh needed to insist on Lalit Shukla's removal from the party presidentship. By April 1985, his relationship with Shukla reached a nadir and it seemed that the I.L.S. President would break all ties with the Swantantra Sangh. Rajesh Pahwa knew that without the S.S.'s support his party would be a non-entity. He led a group of Shukla followers who switched over to the Deshmukh-Kishen Kumar camp. Their exodus broke Shukla's back forcing him to step down in favour of Kishen Kumar.

Short and plump Kishen Kumar had been a S.S. man all his life, starting from being a *Shakha* meeting organiser in rural Rajasthan. He had rapidly progressed to become a full-time S.S. propagandist. The S.S. leadership noticed his organisational brilliance and in 1974, at the age of forty, he was made propaganda secretary of the I.L.S. His loyalty to the S.S. and organisational skills made him the ideal president for the routed I.L.S. Rajesh's background and timely switchover from Shukla helped him build an excellent rapport with the new president. Kumar knew about Rajesh's capacity to mobilise funds and appointed him the new treasurer of the party.

Kishen Kumar wanted the party to gain legitimacy in the eyes of the wealthy, educated sections of society. 'We need persons like your friend Kabir Sabarwal to join the party,' he told Pahwa.

Pahwa replied carefully, 'I am not sure if he wants to come out openly in our support.'

'I want to make him a member of our National Committee. If he still refuses, then you tell him that it is the order of the old man in Thane.'

The September 1985, I.L.S. conclave in Bombay was the first attended by Kabir. He was impressed by the attendance, not knowing that S.S. cadres in plain clothes had been asked to fill up the stadium. Kabir formally joined the party and gave a nervous speech thanking the party and its new president. After Kabir had addressed the conclave, Kishen announced his appointment to the National Committee.

At the end of the conclave, all thirty members the National Committee went to Thane to seek Deshmukh's blessings. After they had all touched the patraich's feet, he addressed them, 'I am sure that under Kishen's leadership, your party will rebuild its image and regain its political base. But one thing still hampers the growth of both the I.L.S. and the S.S. We have always represented the higher castes of Hindus. I want all of us to work to broaden the base of our organisations. Every Hindu should be united under our banner. For that to be possible, we need a mass movement, which touches the soul of every Hindu in India. We need emotive issue for such a movement. Do any of you have any suggestions?'

'We could raise the issue of cow slaughter,' said N N Rao, the only South Indian in the National Committee.

'That is too stale an issue. I want something dramatic, something that will help us whip up Hindu religious sentiments like never before,' said Deshmukh.

As everyone kept silent, Kishen said, 'Deshmukh *ji,* whenever such an issue comes to our mind, we will me back to Thane to receive further instructions.'

Kabir returned from Bombay three days after the newspapers had printed the astonishing news of his joining the I.L.S. Kabir was expecting a big showdown with his father on arrival. But Khem Chand's reaction surprised him. The Lala kept silent on the issue and just asked him, 'How was your trip to Bombay?'

'Successful,' replied Kabir.

'Go meet the girls. They are eagerly awaiting the gifts you must have bought for them.'

Deepika was a growing twelve-year-old. She was a splitting image of her beautiful mother and a brilliant student. While she adored her grandfather and mother, sensing the cold indifference in her father, she kept away from him. She was old enough to understand that her grandfather was very disturbed because of Kabir's Bombay trip. She carefully read the newspaper report on his joining the I.L.S. The report expressed surprise that the son of a secularist and prominent Congress supporter had chosen to join a right wing Hindu party. Deepika became angry with her father for he had gone against her grandfather. On his arrival, he handed her a large box saying, 'This is for you.' She accepted it and didn't say a word.

For Kabir, his second daughter was the person he loved the most in his family. She had her father's prominent facial features and looked very cute. As soon as she saw him, she ran into his outstretched arms. Kabir picked her up and kissed both her cheeks.

'Papa, I really missed you. What have you got for me?'

Kabir laughed at the childish greed he saw in her beautiful eyes. 'Bhagyashree, don't be so impatient. Here are your presents,' he said pointing to three large packets held by a servant.

After the girls had slept, Kabir and Radhika were alone in their bedroom. 'Did Daddy *ji* say anything?' asked Radhika.

'No, he kept quite about the whole issue', replied Kabir.

'The day you joined the party, he was very upset. He retired to his room without eating dinner. Even the next day he hardly spoke a word. He seemed lost in his reminiscences,' worried Radhika.

'He is more than seventy years old. This kind of eccentric and lost behaviour is understandable,' said Kabir. 'Tell me, do you approve of my joining the party?'

Radhika was surprised at her husband's query. 'Do you need my approval?' she asked.

'I thought you would be pleased. After all, your father was a prominent Hindu leader.'

'I never liked that aspect of his,' said Radhika before going off to sleep.

Coming out in the open about his political ideology proved to be both a boon and a bane for Kabir. He was pleasantly surprised by the number of S.S. sympathisers among his employees, business associates and the government officials he dealt with. They all congratulated him on his decision and all his work was promptly done.

The non-Hindus among Kabir and Co.'s factories constituted nearly twenty-five per cent of the labour force and they became insecure about their future. The trade unions decided to take advantage of the situation and labour strikes were organised in almost all the factories. It took Kabir nearly four months to reach costly settlements with the Unions and Kabir and Co.'s 1985-86 result was expected to suffer.

Finally, relieved of his labour troubles, Kabir visited the I.L.S. Head Office.

Pahwa was alone in his room going through the papers piled on his desk. He looked at Kabir and said, 'So you have found time to visit the party office. Please be seated. What will you have?'

Kabir sat down, 'Don't make fun of me. Today, I reached a settlement with the Unions, now I have ample time for party work.'

'This calls for a celebration,' exclaimed Pahwa.

'Yes, it certainly does. What should I get for you. Champagne, Scotch, Vodka?'

Pahwa admonished his friend, 'You should not mention the name of these drinks when you are at the office. We will celebrate later. An old friend of ours will accompany us. She is dying to meet you.'

'Who is she?' asked Kabir.

'I thought one never forgets his first sexual experience.'

'You mean Taruna. It has been at least ten years since I last saw her. Where is she?'

'Don't call her by her first name. She is our new Propaganda Secretary.'

Just then, Vipin Sharma, Pahwa's personal secretary entered the room. 'The party president has called National Committee next Friday. There is a rumour that something big is on the agenda.'

Pahwa stood up, 'Kabir, you wait here. I have to discuss something with Kishen *ji.*'

Twenty Five

Rajesh started the proceedings of the National Committee meeting. 'Deshmukh *ji* had instructed all of us to find an issue, which touches the soul of all Hindus irrespective of the caste to which they belong. It gives me great pleasure in announcing that Kishen Kumar *ji* has found such an issue.'

Kishen Kumar stood up to address his party's top brass. 'Last night I spoke to Deshmukh *ji* and he has approved my idea as it concerns the most revered and idealistic incarnation of Vishnu *ji*, Lord Rama. As you all must be aware, at the Lord's birthplace in Ayodhya stands the Ram Janambhoomi-Babri Masjid site. For decades, because of the dispute, Hindu organisations have been unable to construct a temple at the site. Now is the right time for us to exploit this issue and built it up into a mass movement against the Muslims.'

Lalit Shukla, the former party president interrupted, 'But there is one matter we must consider before launching a movement. While all concerned are sure that Ayodhya town is the birthplace of Lord Rama, archaeologists are not sure whether the disputed site is the exact place where He was born.'

Kishen had been expecting Shukla to raise this point. 'Shukla *ji*, from today please do not refer to the site as a disputed one. For us, it is a temple and nothing else. As for whether the site is the Lord's place or not, the S.S. is soon going to start an enquiry by its own panel of archaeologists.'

'There is another aspect we have to consider,' said N N Rao, 'several independent Hindu organisations are already agitating over the issue.'

'I have discussed this with Deshmukh *ji* and he has agreed to call a conclave of all Hindu organisations and decide on a joint action plan. All these organisations accept the supremacy of the Swatantra Sangh and will listen to Deshmukh *ji*', said Kishen confidently.

'But how will we benefit from all this?' asked Shukla.

'All other organisations, including the S.S. are not political parties. If any of their leaders are desirous of contesting elections, they will have to use our symbol. We stand to gain the most from any movement because we are the only national political party participating,' replied Kishen.

'I hope there is no major communal flare up the movement,' said the National Committee member from Orissa.

'All non-Hindus will be taught a lesson that their future generations will never forget. There won't be any riots, just a crushing of all opposition to our movement. We will herald the revivalism of Hindu militancy like never before. Our new slogan is: *Come what may, we will construct Temple at Ayodhya*,' said Kishen Kumar passionately.

Rajesh Pahwa stood up and started repeating his leader's slogan. The other members followed him vociferously.

*

More than hundred Hindu fundamentalist organisations attended the Ram Janambhoomi conclave in Thane, called by Deshmukh. The entire National Committee of the I.L.S. rubbed shoulders with Hindu rabble-rousers and Sadhus across the country in three days of deliberations. Contentious issues were sorted out and momentous decisions reached.

For Kishen Kumar, the conclave was a huge success. It was unanimously accepted that the I.L.S. would be the only political party to participate in the movement. An eleven member co-ordination committee was set up. An architectural plan for the proposed temple was cleared and nation-wide fund collection drive for its construction was ordered. A team of S.S. archaeologists was formed to conduct an investigation into the site's origins. Several provocative slogans were coined for the movement. It was also decided that since the S.S. was the only organisation having a wide grassroots base, it would lead the movement in the villages and blocks.

The co-ordinated efforts of the fundamentalists succeeded beyond Kishen Kumar's wildest dreams. In just a few months, their activists in every village and town of India shouted provocative war cries in support of a temple at the disputed site. An image of Lord Rama behind bars was shown across the country. The message was clear - 'Hinduism is in danger. Your God is behind bars. Rise up against the Muslims and free your God.' The ranks of the movement were swelling. Hindus from all walks of life were successfully instigated to take on the government and the Muslims.

Kabir was at the forefront of the Indian Lok Sangh's role in the movement. He had contributed a huge amount to the movement's coffers and was now working with Taruna Singh, the I.L.S. Propaganda Secretary. Taruna had aged gracefully and for Kabir she was as beautiful as she had been seventeen years ago. They were both once again attracted to each other and revived their liaison.

Kabir's job was to pinpoint events, which could bring much needed publicity to the movement and send signals that a massive militant Hindu revival was on the cards. It was his suggestion that in terrorism stricken Punjab, the fundamentalist brigades carry small *trishuls* and wear saffron headbands in order to assert their religious identity. When in a meeting Kishen Kumar pointed out that the movement was weakest in Kerala and that there was no knowledge of it, especially in the states rural areas, Kabir presented an ingenuous idea. 'Next week the Pope will be visiting Kerala. If our limited cadre in the state can unitedly demonstrate on his arrival, it will receive wide media coverage and get us the much-needed publicity.'

'But our movement isn't against the Christians,' said Taruna.

'Wherever Hinduism is in danger, we have to defend it. I like Kabir's idea. Ask our Kerala state president to put it into immediate effect,' said Kishen Kumar.

In just a few months, the S.S. led Hindu juggernaut was moving at top speed. In April 1987, Deshmukh and Kishen Kumar decided to display their newly acquired strength. A massive congregation of its activists took place in Ayodhya. Speaker after speaker extolled the one lac activists to continue their work of uprooting the *invaders* and *liberating* Hindu religious sites.

★

The Janaki-Lajwanti Foundation had expanded considerably under Khem Chand's supervision. He had also started a much-needed mobile hospital service in western Uttar Pradesh. Small villages of the region were serviced by a team of doctors who toured the area, spending a day at each place. Khem Chand often accompanied the doctors on their rounds. Deepika aspired to become a doctor and at times, she too came along.

The frenzy over the Ayodhya issue was causing the communal cauldron to boil over throughout Uttar Pradesh and a major flare-up was just waiting to happen.

On 18 May, in Meerut, an insignificant property dispute culminated into one of the worst riots in the country's history. As Hindus and Muslims clashed all over the town, unaware of the riots, Khem Chand and Deepika reached the town en route to Delhi. It was late in the evening and the car was on the busy Delhi-Meerut road. Khem Chand was surprised by the lack of activity. 'There seems to be something wrong,' he told Deepika. Suddenly from a by-lane a mob of thirty came onto the road. Shouting Hindu slogans they stopped at a closed shop on the roadside just fifty metres from the Lala's car. They were standing on the road as two of them tried to break the lock on the shutter. Khem Chand looked at the signboard above the shutter. It was a Muslim tailor's shop. Khem Chand's driver mistakenly honked for the mob to give way. 'Stop you, fool,' Khem Chand rebuked him, but it was too late. The rioters turned to look at the car. Some of them came towards it and they were surrounded. Deepika was shaking with fright and clinged to her grandfather, trying to hide her face in his shirt. A tall wiry man with a saffron headband asked them, 'Are you Hindus?'

The driver was also sweating profusely and in a wavering voice he answered, 'Yes, we are Hindus.'

The man looked at Khem Chand. 'Teach your driver some manners. We are doing important work and he disturbs us by pressing the horn,' he said menacingly.

'I am very sorry,' apologised the driver.

The rioters had broken the lock and opened the shutter. The men surrounding the car returned to the shop and began to pour kerosene from a can onto the shop's contents. Just as they were about to light a match, a large mob of Muslims entered the road from the opposite street. Like the Hindu mob, they too were armed with swords and spears. Both the groups were equally matched in numbers and arms and stood just fifty metres apart. For almost a minute, neither group moved as if frightened to take on the other. Then the leader of the Hindus shouted their war cry, 'Come what may, we will construct the temple at Ayodhya.' His followers passionately repeated his words and rushed towards their adversaries. The Muslim mob also readied their weapons and moved forward. A terrible free-for-all ensued.

Khem Chand shook his horror-stricken driver, 'Be calm. As quietly as possible try to U-turn the car.'

The driver wiped his sweaty forehead and carefully followed Khem Chand's order. As the car was almost completely turned, some of the rioters noticed that it was going to escape. Shouting loudly they ran towards it. The Lala saw them coming and shouted, 'They have seen us. Step on the accelerator.' The driver pressed the accelerator hard. The car gained speed just as the rioters were on to it. One of them struck the rear window with his sword. Deepika screamed as the shattered safety glass pieces fell on her hair and shoulders. The car gained more speed and the rioters were unable to follow. After travelling for a few minutes, the Lala carefully removed the pieces of glass from Deepika's body. She was shaken up but unhurt.

Twenty Six

Khem Chand and Deepika returned home safe and sound. As he recounted their lucky escape, Radhika tightly hugged her elder daughter. Kabir commented nonchalantly, 'All's well that ends well.'

'We were lucky to escape but what about the hundreds who won't escape. Your party has raised this sensitive issue and caused these riots,' blamed Khem Chand.

It was the first time that the Lala had mentioned Kabir's connection to the I.L.S. Kabir replied firmly, 'What my party does isn't your headache.'

A couple of days later, Kabir received an early morning phone call from Rajesh. 'The party president wants you in his office within an hour.'

As he was seated in front of Kishen Kumar, the party president said, 'Kabir, we have a big problem on our hands. In the Meerut riots, both sides were equally matched and suffered almost identical casualties. Yesterday morning, I decided to send some of our most violent activists to wreck havoc on the Muslims in order to boost our Hindu brothers in the town. A batch of forty activists took up positions in the S.S. dharmashala and houses of our party men. But curfew was clamped and they are trapped in their hideouts.'

'When curfew is lifted, they will be able to return. What is the problem?' asked Kabir.

'The police is soon going to conduct house-to-house searches and look for hidden weapons. Our men are bound to be discovered. Most of them are office bearers of our party and the S.S. If they are caught with their weapons, it will be just the excuse needed by the government to ban all our activities,' explained Kishen. 'You have a factory on the edge of Meerut town. If they take shelter in your premises, they will be saved from the searches.'

'I will try my best,' assured Kabir.

The chief of security at Kabir's Meerut factory was a robust ex-police inspector, Lalit Singh. He was surprised when he received Kabir's personal call. 'Sir, this is an honour,' he said proudly.

Kabir explained in detail what he wanted him to accomplish. 'But sir, if the police is conducting the searches, they will also be at our factory,' said Singh.

'They are searching houses, not closed factories. Do this job well and you will be rewarded,' said Kabir.

Lalit Singh knew that following Kabir's risky instructions would ensure a prosperous future for him. He had lived in Meerut all his life and carefully planned the route from the men's hideout to the factory. By nightfall, the forty men were safely encamped in Kabir's factory.

Kishen Kumar was pleased with Kabir's work. 'We are all very grateful to you,' he said.

'When you need to bring them out of Meerut, just tell me,' said Kabir.

'I have planned some special work for them before they return.'

Maliana was a cluster of small villages just five kilometres from Meerut. It had 35,000 residents, ten per cent of whom were Muslims. On the afternoon of 23 May, Kishen's platoon of forty men reached the villages. Local S.S. men had prior knowledge of their arrival and welcomed them. Soon a large mob gathered and began burning down Muslim houses. To compound the carnage, the police joined the mob. In just two hours, scores of Muslim houses and business establishments had been destroyed. Over fifty persons lay dead, killed by the police and fundamentalists.

A week after the Maliana carnage, normalcy slowly returned. Khem Chand decided it was time to restart the mobile medical facility in and around Meerut and personally supervised its return.

The medical team was treating patients at a locality on the outskirts of Meerut when a tall burly man approached Khem Chand.

'Lala *ji*, do you recognise me?' he asked.

Khem Chand tried to remember the bearded middle-aged

Muslim.

'I am sorry, I don't recognise you,' said Khem Chand.

'I was just ten when you saved my life. I am Khalil, son of Sadat Khan.'

Khem Chand stood up and joyfully hugged him.

'I should have recognised you. Your appearance is very similar to that of your father. How is he?'

'He passed away last year,' said Khalil.

'I am sorry to hear that. Your father was a strong leader of the community.'

Khalil acknowledged the Lala's condolences and said. 'I came here just to meet you. There is something serious I want to talk about.'

They slowly walked away from the medical team and sat down in the shade of a mango tree.

'Lala *ji,* I know you are an honourable man, who despite suffering personal tragedies have never given up the principle of secularism. But your son has become an active player in a very dangerous game,' said Khalil gravely.

'What has he done?' asked the Lala.

'About fifty Hindu fanatics came to Meerut from outside. They would have been arrested but they were given shelter at your company's factory. Later on, these very men led the mob which ravaged Maliana.'

The Lala's body went numb and tears started flowing from his eyes. He asked, 'Are you absolutely sure about this?'

Khalil felt Khem Chand's sorrow. He put his hand on the Lala's shoulder. 'Lala *ji*, I would have never told you about this, if I wasn't sure. However, you can confirm my story from the security staff at the factory.'

An hour later, Khem Chand's car was at the factory gate. It had not reopened after the riots and only the security staff was available. Khem Chand's driver told them that Lala *ji* wanted to meet their chief. Lalit Singh rushed to the car, hands folded in respect.

'Sir, I have heard so much about you,' he said.

Khem Chand said curtly, 'Get in the car.'

As Lalit Singh sat on the front seat, Khem Chand demanded, 'I want you to tell me everything about the unexpected guests who stayed in the factory. If you lie, I promise that I will ensure that you are kicked out from this job.'

The command in the Lala's voice surprised Lalit Singh. 'Sir, I just followed Kabir *ji's* orders. He asked me to take them out of the residential area and arrange for their stay in the factory.'

'When did they leave?' asked Khem Chand.

'They left on the 23 May, at about twelve. I remember clearly because that was the day the Maliana massacre took place.'

Twenty Seven

It was eleven p.m. and the Lala was all alone in the bungalow. The servants had gone off to sleep. Only the watchman was awake. Radhika and the girls were in Ludhiana for a relative's wedding. Khem Chand had become tired of waiting for Kabir to return and had begun to write in his diary. Since Lajo's death whenever he was troubled, he translated his feelings into words and wrote them in the diary.

Khem Chand was about to finish writing when he heard Kabir's car come in. Slowly, he locked the dairy into his desk drawer and walked to the staircase. As Kabir climbed up the stairs he was surprised to see his father standing at the top.

'Up till so late,' he commented.

'I want to speak to you,' said Khem Chand. The gravity in his voice caused Kabir to follow him. On entering his bedroom, Khem Chand sat down in his armchair and said, 'Sit down. What I have to say will take some time.'

'I hope it doesn't take too long,' said Kabir looking at his watch, 'tomorrow I have an early morning meeting.'

The Lala kept staring at him, not wanting an acrimonious argument. Kabir followed his father's order to sit down.

'I know about your involvement in the Meerut riots. I know that you used the factory to shelter your fellow fascists. Your irresponsible actions have once again endangered the future of this family and the business. It seems your party men have brainwashed all sense from your brain,' said the Lala angrily.

Kabir realised that there was no point in defending and went on the offensive.

'My party men are not fascists. They are true Hindus who want to construct a temple at the birthplace of Lord Rama. The Muslims are opposing the construction and hence they have to be taught a lesson,' he said passionately.

'There are hundreds of sacred temples and shrines across the country. I have never seen you visit even one of them. In fact, it has been years since you have visited the temple in our neighbourhood. Now you are all worked up about constructing a temple at the disputed side. Your party is just using the issue to gain politically,' said the Lala.

'Only a coward like you can say these words. You did not avenge the deaths of your wife and sons, instead you chose to marry a widow half your age,' shouted Kabir.

'How dare you be disrespectful towards Lajo? She loved you like a son, she craved for your attention. She always covered your every mistake,' said the Lala emotionally.

Kabir refused to acknowledge Lajo's love for him and said, 'You were a victim of Partition. But you never supported the Swatantra Sangh or the I.L.S. Can't you understand that we want to rid this country of all Muslims, they should all be sent to Pakistan.'

'You are talking about organisations that thrive on misinformation and rumours. Traditionally, Hinduism is the most secular religion in the world. But your canards are causing militancy among Hindus. Have you ever thought how can India's eighty per cent Hindus ever be threatened by any minority community?' reasoned Khem Chand.

'Perhaps your knowledge of current affairs is not as good as it used to be. We may be in majority but everywhere we are being persecuted. This has caused many to join in our fight. Every day policemen, civil servants, sportsmen and intellectuals are joining us. The moment is not far when we will capture power at the centre,' said Kabir proudly.

'You were part of the 1977 government and look what happened to it. Your party's ideology was one the major factor for its disintegration. A narrow-minded ideology like yours will never be able to administrate our vast and diverse country. There is still time for you to change. Till your college life you never discriminated between a Hindu and a Muslim. Your best friend was a Muslim boy. What changed all that?' said Khem Chand desperately trying to convince his son.

Kabir replied vehemently, 'He was a back stabber like all of his faith. You remember his death? It was not an accident. I killed him and that half-foreign bitch. I killed them and I will continue to do so till this country is rid of all Muslims. I have to avenge the death of my mother and brothers.'

Kabir's maniacal words and the homicidal gleam in his eyes stunned the Lala into silence. Kabir stood up and left the room.

'Stop, Kabir. I have something to tell you. It is very important. Please stop,' said the Lala. But Kabir had left the room. Khem Chand stood up to go after him. A sharp pain gripped the left side of his upper body. His heart felt as if a sharp dagger had been plunged straight into it. Clutching his chest, the Lala tried to steady himself but he went down. As he fell on the carpet he tried to shout for help but no words came out. His eyelids seemed to weigh a ton and he closed them. Through his closed eyes he saw deceased family members calling out to him. Janaki, his two sons and Lajo were all beckoning him to join them.

Then the pain seemed to recede and he saw a brightly-lit tunnel opening for him.

Kabir made the Lala's funeral into a major political event. The body was not cremated for two days to facilitate the arrival of all top Hindu right wing leaders. Radhika protested but she was silenced by her husband. A huge tent was erected outside the bungalow as hundreds of Kabir and Co. employees and political activists came to pay their last respects to Lala Khem Chand Sabarwal.

On the day of the cremation, the body draped in the I.L.S. flag, was put atop a large carriage. Kabir, along with the S.S. chief Deshmukh, I.L.S. president Kishen Kumar, Rajesh Pahwa and prominent Sadhus and right wing leaders stood on the carriage as it began its journey to the Nigambodh Ghat. Thousands walked along, accompanying the Lala on his last journey.

Every part of the Ghat was filled by mourners as Kabir performed the last rites. He lit the pyre and a few minutes later left the cremation area. In just an hour the Ghat was once again deserted except for one man. Sanjeev Khanna stood near the pyre silently, tears continuously pouring from his eyes and he kept shaking his head.

Twenty Eight

The Swatantra Sangh led movement had grown remarkably by 1989. The I.L.S. and the S.S. notched success after success, their coffers now held hundreds of crores and their ranks had swelled beyond all expectations. With opposition unity once again a possibility, they were sure to be active players in any new dispensation at the centre. Attendance at the Swatantra Sangh's weekly *Shakha* meetings had increased manifold and these had once again become handy tools to defame and discredit the ruling party.

Kabir's relationship with Radhika and Deepika had deteriorated considerably since the Lala's death. In the last two years, Radhika had become distant and listless towards him. Husband and wife hardly ever discussed anything. They only talked when it was absolutely necessary. Deepika refused to forgive her father for turning her grandfather's death into a political circus. All communication between father and daughter had ceased ever since. Several times Kabir brought this up with Radhika. 'She doesn't even wish me anymore, you should teach her to respect me.'

'She idolised her grandfather and you used his death to achieve political ends. She knows how much Lala *ji* hated your party men and their ideology. She will never forgive you,' was Radhika's reply.

Kabir had never liked his elder daughter. He continued to shower all his affection and love on his younger daughter. Bhagyashree was now ten and she reciprocated his feelings. Whatever little time Kabir had to spare from his busy business and political schedule, was spent with her. He took her to picnics, amusement parks and historical landmarks in and around Delhi. Kabir spoke at length about his movement. Knowing that Bhayashree could comprehend little, he tried to explain their ideology as simply as he could. He believed in the S.S. policy of catching them young and wanted his daughter to follow in his political footsteps.

Kabir and Co. Ltd. had registered healthy growth rates and because of splits in other business houses, it was now the fifth largest in the country. Kabir had also found his 'Sanjeev Khanna.' Deepak Chaturvedi was a brilliant young executive and even though he had started his career with a leading multinational, he was a staunch supporter of the S.S.'s *Swadeshi* policy.

Since Khem Chand's death, Kabir had also reorganised the Janaki-Lajwanti Foundation. He had first renamed it the Sabarwal Foundation and then changed its line of charitable work. The Foundation now concentrated solely on providing accommodation and health care to pilgrims in all major Hindu religious centres. Large facilities were constructed in Varanasi, Ayodhya, Haridwar and Mathura. The work of the Foundation was appreciated by all components of the S.S. family and Kabir was felicitated by one of the S.S.'s frontal organisations.

Politically, Kabir had become very powerful within the S.S. family. In 1988, he was appointed Chairman of the Indian Lok Sangh's Economic Department, which had for decades espoused *Swadeshi* thinking. Kabir managed to convince some fellow industrialists to publicly support his line of thinking and that provided a fresh impetus to the cause of *Swadeshi*. Kabir had also become very popular with the cadres of the S.S. family. All leaders and activists who came to him for financial help never went back disappointed.

Under the tutelage of a senior S.S. functionary, Kabir had once again honed his public speaking skills. He had since become a popular speaker at the movement's public meetings and sessions. Kabir's style was different from the rabble rousers in the movement. He spoke in a firm voice and laced his speeches with hard-hitting facts and figures.

In just three years of active politics, Kabir had almost completely overshadowed Rajesh Pahwa. Their friendship had endured despite this but now Pahwa seemed to be stonewalling Kabir's attempts to find a suitable constituency for contesting the ensuing Lok Sabha polls.

There were rumours that Pahwa himself was facing political

problems. It was said that Deshmukh was cross with him over one of his speeches. Pahwa had called for a merger of all opposition parties without any authorisation from Deshmukh or Kishen Kumar. Pahwa had recently started openly hobnobbing with other opposition leaders and his statement was seen as a result of that. Deshmukh and Kishen were both against a repeat of 1977. They only wanted to align with opposition parties and not merge with them. Hence, they were peeved with Pahwa.

Knowing that even if the rumours were true, he was no match for Pahwa's manipulative skills. Kabir decided to take up the matter directly with the old man in Thane.

They met in the same hall where Kabir had, on the completion of office training, received the blessings of the previous S.S. chief, K B Patel. Deshmukh stood up as Kabir touched his feet. As they sat down, the old man said him, 'We were going to meet at the upcoming conclave in Hyderabad. So you must have come all this way to discuss an important issue.'

Kabir said, 'Deshmukh *ji*, I have loyally served the S.S. for two decades. I rightfully want a suitable constituency for myself. But my own friend Rajesh Pahwa is creating obstacles in my path.'

Deshmukh smiled, 'Pahwa has become too ambitious for his own good. Anyway, he is neither the Swatantra Sangh chief nor the I.L.S. President. You are the brightest star in our galaxy. Hundreds of Rajesh Pahwas cannot stop your rise in national politics.'

The patriarch's words encouraged Kabir. 'Then I can choose a constituency for myself,' asked Kabir.

'You should not risk your future by contesting a mere Lok Sabha election. I have great plans for your future. Your appointment as Chairman of the Economic Department was my idea. The future belongs to articulate and intelligent politicians like you. Publicly acknowledged hard-liners like Kishen may never be able to reach the top. We need a wolf in sheep's clothing and you are the best one we have got. You are just forty-two and if you follow the directions from Thane, who knows, one day you might even become the Prime Minister of India. As for the present, the next time the I.L.S. has a Rajya Sabha seat, I promise it will be yours.

Twenty Nine

Ten years ago, when Sanjeev Khanna had left Kabir and Co. all he had was a small house in West Delhi and a few thousand rupees in his bank. But he had helped found one of the biggest conglomerates in the country and he received dozens of excellent job offers. Out of all these, he accepted the post of Vice President at India MSW Ltd., one of the largest multinationals operating the country. India MSW produced a range of soaps, toothpastes, shampoos, hair oils and talcum powders. Its products were used in almost every middle class Indian household and its brands were among the most valuable in the country.

In spite of being European owned, India MSW had always been headed by an Indian. The company had produced some of the best executives and marketing experts in the country. Its business strategy was both feared and respected by its competitors.

Sanjeev Khanna adjusted quickly to the professional management style of the company and excelled in his work. By 1985, he had spent six extremely successful years at the company and was promoted to the post of Executive Director with specific charge of mergers and acquisitions. Khanna soon came to be called the 'Takeover Executive', as acting on his advice MSW bought half a dozen companies. The new acquisitions proved immensely successful and were consequently merged into India MSW. In 1989, Khanna was appointed the company's Chief Executive Officer.

Being a bachelor, Khanna had led a lonely life. His only passion, hobby and recreation was his work. Sanjeev's nature was such that he never forgot a favour and never forgave a slight. Kabir had dishonoured him, abused him and taken away his thirty-year-old job. Sanjeev had curbed his anger out of his immense love and respect for the Lala. Khem Chand's death had affected him deeply. The one man who had given him a golden opportunity at a very young age and changed his whole life was now dead. Since his death, Sanjeev had been waiting for an opportunity to settle scores with Kabir.

On a cold November morning, he was thinking of precisely that when his Vice President walked into the office.

'Sir, there is a matter I need to discuss with you,' he said.

Sanjeev motioned for him to sit down. The Vice President said, 'Sir, as you know it is likely that the opposition will form the next government at the centre. I had told you earlier about the attacks on shopkeepers who stock our goods. The Indian Lok Sangh and Swatantra Sangh ordered these attacks. We are receiving reports that when the new government is in office, these attacks will increase in intensity and number. We have to do something.'

'You reported twenty such attacks in the western states over a period of six months. Our products are very popular. How can a few more incidents affect our overall sales?' asked Khanna disinterestedly.

'Sir, *Swadeshi* is one of the major election planks of the I.L.S. Ever since Kabir Sabarwal took over as its Economic Department Chairman, he has been demanding a boycott of all goods produced by multinationals. You must have heard about the new name he has coined for multinationals. He calls them 'the East India Companies of the future.'

Sanjeev was suddenly very interested in his Vice President's words. 'What do you suggest, we should do?' he asked.

'Sir, we have to take these pseudo-*Swadeshis* head on. I think we should engage a professional agency to formulate a strategy.'

'I like your idea. Set up a meeting for me with the chief of International Detective Agency and Security Services. I have heard that it is the leader in its field,' said Sanjeev.

The chief of the Agency was Tarun Banerjee, one of the most respected investigators in the country. The meeting took place in Banerjee's lavish office in Connaught Place. The opulence and size of the office surprised Khanna.

'Even I don't have an office like yours,' he said.

Banerjee laughed loudly. 'I always wanted a huge office. Thirty years ago, when I started as an investigator in this agency, I had such a small cabin that even one visitor could hardly sit in it.

Now can we discuss your problem?' said Banerjee.

Banerjee carefully wrote down all that Sanjeev said. After Sanjeev had finished, Banerjee said, 'Mr Khanna, if we are to solve this problem I need your total support and an unlimited budget.'

After Sanjeev had agreed, Banerjee continued, 'There is one thing you must understand. These people are unscrupulous politicians. To gain political mileage, they will go to any length. There is a strong possibility that once they are in power, these methods will be used not just for political gains but also to extort money from your company. To prevent that we have to take them on aggressively.'

'How will we do that?' asked Sanjeev.

'Politicians are human beings like us and they have human weaknesses. We have extensive records on almost all the leading politicians. My men will dig into those records and try to find something you can use,' said Banerjee.

Kabir was liberally used by the I.L.S. for election campaigning. All through the campaign period he moved from one election meeting to another propagating the ideals of the Hindu right, the essentiality of the Ayodhya Temple and *Swadeshi*. The combined opposition managed to get more seats than the Congress party. The I.L.S. chose to stay out of the government supporting it from outside.

While the party's tally in the Lok Sabha increased substantially, Pahwa was defeated by a huge margin from his constituency in Delhi. He had paid dearly for his independent actions. The entire S.S. cadre had sabotaged his election campaign and polling process. The S.S.'s *Matdaan* wing founded by his late father polled bogus votes. But not for him, they voted en masse for his main opponent. Pahwa's third successive defeat caused his influence to wane considerably. In the S.S. and I.L.S. circles, he was now considered a spent force, a man with no political future.

Kabir's popularity within the I.L.S. continued to grow after the elections. On Deshmukh's instructions. Kishen Kumar made him a general secretary of the party. A number of sensitive states were under his charge and he used them to expand his support base.

Kabir was elected to the Rajya Sabha in March 1990. He was

confident that Deshmukh's prophecy would definitely come true. Newspaper reports described him as the most powerful Punjabi in the country. Kabir's immediate goal was to become the I.L.S. President, as Kishan Kumar's term would be over within a year. Deshmukh had publicly blessed his bid for party presidentship. This discouraged other claimants to come forward.

Kabir was getting increasingly delusional. All he thought about was how and when he would take over as the country's Prime Minister. He had even begun preparing a list of the measures he would undertake with regards to the status of minorities in India. Kabir's perverted ideology made him think that his acts against minorities would make him the greatest Prime Minister ever.

Kabir's delusions about his future made him extremely security conscious. In order to beef up his security, he contacted R K Singh, a former Director General of Police and a prominent I.L.S. supporter. Singh was presently training a team of five hundred activists. They were being taught about explosives and arms.

The first flaw Singh picked up in Kabir's security was his bungalow.

'A five hundred square yard house can never be safe. You need a much bigger house,' he said.

Since Kabir's Member of Parliament status entitled him to just a small apartment, he decided to buy a new house.

Thirty

Attacks on multinational companies and their products were increasing manifold. As India MSW's products were the most visible, it was being hit the hardest. Shopkeepers stocking their goods were beaten up in public and godowns of their distributors ransacked. Pressure was mounting on Sanjeev Khanna to find a way out. One of his directors had even suggested paying bribes to silence the S.S. and I.L.S. But Sanjeev had refused to bow down to the pressure tactics.

It had been nine months since he had contracted Tarun Banerjee's agency. Banerjee had given him scandalous information on several second rung I.L.S. leaders but nothing on Kabir Sabarwal. Losing patience Sanjeev decided to give Tarun an ultimatum.

'After nine months of extensive investigations, you haven't produced anything I can use against Kabir Sabarwal. You have one more month, after that I will rescind your contract,' he said.

'Mr Khanna, our records list an investigation about Kabir Sabarwal in 1964.' Sanjeev interrupted him, 'What is it about?'

'There is a problem. All reports of 1964 have been misplaced. As soon as we are able to trace them, I am sure we will have something useful,' said Banerjee.

Kabir had bought a huge bungalow in Delhi's Punjabi Bagh area. It required renovations and he planned to move within a month. The only problem was that Radhika and Deepika had ganged up and refused to leave the old house. 'I have fond memories of this house. I came here as a young bride. Daddy *ji* treasured this house. He personally tended the garden. I want to stay here till the day I die,' she said firmly. Even though Deepika did not speak to her father, she indicated that she shared her mother's views. Bhagyashree had been initially excited about the new house, but Deepika had convinced her that they shouldn't leave. Now she too was against moving.

Kabir desperately tried to convince his wife but all his efforts proved futile. Now that he was in the centre stage of national politics, Kabir did not want to move without his family. Staying alone would cause irreparable damage to his family man image and adversely affect his political future. Tired of trying to convince her, Kabir decided to threaten her.

'I won't sell this house if you agree to move. It will be maintained in its present state and you can visit at weekends. However, if you continue to oppose me I promise that I will sell this house and then your fond memories will be lost forever,' he said sarcastically. Knowing that her husband would carry out his threat, Radhika was forced to comply.

Kabir was in a meeting with his architect, when his secretary entered the office. 'Sir, your party secretary just called. You have an important meeting at the party office at nine p.m.'

The I.L.S. headquarter was deserted at the late hour except for security guards. Kabir went straight to Kishan Kumar's office. The I.L.S. secretary was outside the president's door.

'They are waiting for you,' he said opening the door. Entering the office he saw Deshmukh and Kishen Kumar engrossed in discussion. Kabir closed the door and before sitting he touched the patriarch's feet.

'Kabir, you are five minutes late. Sit down. A serious matter has to be discussed,' he said curtly. Kabir could feel the tension in the patriarch's voice.

'A very serious problem has arisen. The government's decision to enforce the recommendations of the Mandal Commission is an attempt to divide the Hindus. Our support base will be divided if we do not give a befitting reply,' Kabir suggested.

'We can always withdraw support and bring down the government,' he suggested.

'In the present situation, such an action will only benefit the Congress and hasten its return to power. Eventually, we will withdraw our support but before that a lot has to be accomplished,' said Kishan Kumar.

'It seems that you have something planned,' said Kabir.

Kishan Kumar was about to reply but was stopped by Deshmukh. The Swatantra Sangh Chief looked straight into

Kabir's eyes. 'You are going to take over as the I.L.S. President in just three months. Your future is bound to be affected by all this. How do you plan to counter the Mandal Commission?' asked Deshmukh.

Kabir knew that he was being tested and paused to carefully consider his reply. Slowly he said, 'Deshmukh *ji*, in my S.S. training in Thane, I was taught a principle I have used all my life. If your opponent tries to cow you down, respond with an even greater force and do not stop till you subjugate him. We have to use the same principle to prevent division in our support base. We will start communal riots like never before and create anarchy all over the country. We will concentrate on Congress ruled states to prevent it from taking any advantage. After that our vast propaganda network will spread the message that ordinary people's safety cannot be ensured by a Congress or ruling combine's administration. All parties except ours will be totally discredited. Then we shall withdraw support and call for fresh Lok Sabha elections.'

As soon as Kabir finished speaking, Deshmukh exclaimed, 'Bravo, bravo! You are a true S.S. man. Your ideas are similar to what we had decided before your arrival. We had also decided that you would lead the entire campaign against this issue. You have our full support, implement your ideas,'

Kabir formulated his dangerous game plan in just a day. A co-ordinated strike on minorities in twelve communally sensitive towns was planned. D' day was to be in two weeks. He personally called S.S. cadres to issue instructions. At the end of each phone call, Kabir said, 'If you have any doubts, check with the old man in Thane.'

He also planned ahead of D' day. An itinerary was fixed for him to address public meetings in all major non-I.L.S. ruled states. At each meeting Kabir would ridicule the administrative capabilities of the state governments. At the end of his tour, a large rally was to be organised in Delhi. There, in front of a huge crowd, Kabir would announce the Indian Lok Sangh's decision to withdraw support because of worsening law and order situation.

Thirty One

In spite of the late hour, there was some traffic on the route from Connaught Place to Kabir's Civil Lines residence. Sanjeev Khanna had waited for years to square his account with Kabir and he was in a hurry to meet him.

'Your fascist political career is over,' he said aloud. Also now he would surely make Kabir stop his vicious campaign against multinationals. Sanjeev felt the paper in his shirt's pocket.

'For you this is not a piece of paper, it is a nuclear bomb. It will devastate not only Kabir Sabarwal, but all the organisations he proudly represents,' Banerjee had said handing him the paper.

Sanjeev's amazement on reading the paper was evident to Banerjee.

'Send the original report to my office,' Sanjeev had managed to say, unable to recover from the shock. As the significance of what he had read began to sink in, tears had come to his eyes thinking about the greatness of Lala Khem Chand Sabarwal. Deciding to waste no time Sanjeev, had driven straight from Banerjee's office to Kabir's house.

The watchman at the bungalow recognised Sanjeev and let him in. He had walked a few steps when two burly men appeared from behind the bushes lining the driveway.

'Who do you want to meet?' asked one of them.

'Tell Kabir, Sanjeev Khanna is here.'

Sanjeev was led to the drawing room and asked to sit.

He had to wait for just a minute when Kabir appeared. Descinding the stairs quickly, he rudely asked 'What do you want?'

'I am here in my official capacity as Chief Executive of India MSW. On behalf of my company, I demand that you stop all…'

Kabir's loud laughter interrupted him.

'You dare to demand anything from me,' he said incredulously. 'Your "East India Company" will be kicked out of this country very soon.

'My company was present in India even before your S.S. or I.L.S. were founded. Your fascist ideology and narrow-minded economic beliefs will cause the decimation of your organisation, while India MSW will continue to flourish,' said Sanjeev refusing to be cowed down by Kabir's rhetoric.

'Get out,' said Kabir shaking with anger.

'Before I leave I want you to read this,' he said, putting the paper in Kabir's hand. Kabir saw the letterhead on the paper and refused to read it. 'This International Detective Agency is owned by anti I.L.S. businessmen. They must have fabricated a story to malign me. Dinesh, Satish, throw this gentlemen out,' he ordered his body guards.

As the two men caught hold of him, Sanjeev shouted, 'Kabir read it and all your conceit will vanish. You will realise who you truly are.'

Kabir laughed once again and started to tear the report into small pieces. Sanjeev tried to free himself from his captors and said, 'You are not Lala *ji's* son. You…' Before he could finish the sentence one of the men punched him in his stomach.

Kabir came over and slapped Sanjeev repeatedly. 'How dare you utter such words!'

The blows stunned Sanjeev. As he started to speak he was once again punched.

'Take him outside, teach him a lesson he won't ever forget,' ordered Kabir.

Kabir woke up early disturbed by the noise in the house. The drawing room furniture was being loaded to be taken to the new house. He saw Radhika ready to leave. 'Where are you going?' he asked rubbing his eyes.

'To the new house, I have to set up this furniture and check out the decor work,' she said putting on her earrings.

'Where is my breakfast?' asked Kabir.

'The servant will get it for you, I am in a hurry. I have to be back before the girls return from school.'

While brushing his teeth, Kabir thought about the last minute preparations before the impending D' day. Radhika's voice interrupted his thoughts. 'Soon, they will be loading the furniture in the bedrooms. Please get it done in your presence,' she said.

Kabir asked the labourers to remove all the furniture in his bedroom except for his desk and chair, leaving them to start their work. Kabir asked the servant to unlock his father's room. He had decided to spend some time in his late father's room. Entering it for the first time since the Lala's death, Kabir sat on his comfortable armchair.

Kabir had an afternoon meeting with Kishen Kumar and was free till then. Casually he started opening the drawers of his father's desk. Finding the top one locked he became curious and looked in the other drawers for its key. Unable to find it, he summoned the servant. 'Get a hammer and open this drawer,' he ordered.

It took just a couple of blows for the lock to break. Sending the servant out of the room he opened the drawer expecting to find some valuables in it. It only contained a thick leather bound diary and a file. Kabir remembered that Radhika had often mentioned about his father's habit of writing in his diary. So this is the diary, he thought.

Suddenly, it crossed his mind that Khem Chand might have written about his involvement in the Meerut riots. Worried that the Lala's writings could incriminate him in the future, he quickly leafed through the yellowed pages. His fears proved correct when on a page he saw the date written by Khem Chand in his neat handwriting - 1st June 1987. Kabir was surprised that just under the date, Khem Chand had written – 'Kabir, I hope one day you will read this because I have written what I could never tell you on your face.'

Kabir comfortably settled into the armchair and began reading.

My dear son,

After the deaths of Janaki and my sons, Chander and Mahesh, I stayed alive because of you. All my efforts were to ensure a good future for you. It is just a quirk of fate that all my business ventures proved so successful. Perhaps, the Almighty was showering His blessings on me because of the trials and tribulations I had to suffer due to the Partition.

I know you despise me because, in spite of suffering terrible personal losses, I refused to lift a finger against any Muslims. My wife and children were not killed by Muslims, they were killed by rioters. I have always believed that rioters do not belong to any religion, they are just rioters. It pains me deeply that you have become similar to those who killed my family.

I am unable to understand what caused such terrible hatred in you. I can be a protective father and say that you are blameless, your friendship with Rajesh Pahwa was to blame. But every man has to be held accountable for his actions. If the men you had hidden in our factory had been discovered, you would have been arrested and not your fascist friends.

I know you strongly resent my calling your party a fascist one, but it is the plain and simple truth. One day, you will realise that what I say is correct. I can only hope that by then you are not so far gone that you are unable to return.

Have you ever thought why I named you Kabir? I gave you this name because I wanted you to be a strong believer in both Hinduism and Islam. I gave you this name because I dreamt that you would dispel all the communal hatred caused by Partition. And I gave you this name because like the Sufi Saint Kabir, you have been born in one faith and have been reared by a man of a different faith.

In spite of the fact that you are not really my son, I have loved you more than I had ever loved my two sons. I constantly pray that God shows you the right path and he dispels all the communal poison these fascists have pumped into your brain.'

Kabir's head spun and he tried to focus his thoughts. A torrent of tears flowed down his cheeks and a thousand unanswered questions came to his mind. Even as his body seemed to freeze, he managed to open the file in the drawer. It contained only one piece of paper. The letterhead read 'International Detective Agency.'

With trembling hands Kabir began to read. When he finished, almost all his questions were answered. His fanatical delusions vanished and he experienced a new clarity in his thoughts. Vivid images filled his mind. A *burkha* clad young woman nursing her newborn son. A wounded, bearded young man handing the same baby to the Lala. The inside of the Mosque he used to visit. Saffron clad Swatantra Sangh teachers training him in their ideology. And then the bodies of the Maliana carnage rotting in the summer heat and floating in a canal, vultures feeding on them.

Slowly Kabir picked himself up, clutching the diary and file in his hand. Entering his bedroom, he placed them on his desk, as it was the only piece of furniture left.

He opened the top drawer and under his personal files, he found what he was looking for. Removing the safety catch, he held the revolver to his forehead.

Kabir looked at the Lala's framed photograph on his desk. Khem Chand's eyes seemed to look lovingly at him. Through his tears, Kabir smiled at his father and pressed the trigger.

Epilogue

Sanjeev had been waiting for five minutes when he was shown into Kishen Kumar's office. The Indian Lok Sangh president looked at him menacingly and motioned for him to sit.

Sanjeev smiled and waited for the politician to speak.

'Khanna *ji*, yesterday we received the paper you sent by courier. I do not know of your motives for doing so, but I am sure that the document had been fabricated to malign the I.L.S. and the memory of our deceased associate, Kabir Sabarwal,' said Kishen Kumar looking Sanjeev straight in the eye.

'Was learning this art a part of your Swatantra Sangh training?' asked Sanjeev cheerfully.

'What art?'

'Looking a person straight in the eye while you are lying,' said Sanjeev.

'Khanna *ji*, you don't know the extent of our power. You better watch your tongue,' said Kishen angrily pointing a finger at Sanjeev.

'Mr Kishen, you understand one thing. We both know that the press is refusing to buy your story that Kabir's death was an accident and not a suicide. I hope you are ready to withstand the repercussions if I send the document to all major newspapers,' said Sanjeev getting up to leave.

Kishen Kumar knew that he had to give in. Last night he had spoken to Deshmukh. The patriarch had shouted on the phone, 'Agree to anything he says. If this gets public, it will cause irreversible damage to our image.'

'What do you want?' Kishen asked Sanjeev.

Smelling victory, Sanjeev put forth his demands. 'I want immediate withdrawal of your call to boycott multinationals. All actions against shopkeepers and distributors are to be halted. Also, I do not want anyone of your party men anywhere near the Sabarwal family or their business.'

With no option but to agree, Kishen sheepishly nodded his head.

Sanjeev drove from the I.L.S. office to the Sabarwal bungalow in Civil Lines. Radhika was waiting for him in the lawn.

'Get me a cup of coffee,' he told the servant standing nearby.

After the servant had left, Radhika asked apprehensively, 'Did they agree to leave us alone?'

'I convinced them,' said Sanjeev.

They sat silently for a couple of minutes and then Radhika said, 'I am glad that those fanatics will be out of our lives. Do you know that Deshmukh wanted me to become a member of the I.L.S?'

'Kabir had become extremely powerful within their organisations. I have heard rumours that he was going to be the next I.L.S. President,' said Sanjeev.

Radhika spoke softly, 'They wanted to use our family name and money to achieve their political objectives.'

'You know that Kabir was no saint himself, he was probably more maniacal than his partymen,' said Sanjeev without mincing any words.

Radhika said, 'Sanjeev *ji*, there is a lot I have to tell you. You probably don't know why Kabir had committed suicide.

Sanjeev interrupted her, 'I know everything. You need not say a word.'